THE FRENCHMAN'S MARRIAGE DEMAND

THE
FRENCHMAN'S
MARRIAGE
DEMAND

BY

CHANTELLE SHAW

MILLS & BOON®

Pure reading pleasure

First published in Great Britain 2007
Large Print edition 2008
Harlequin Mills & Boon Limited,
Eton House, 18-24 Paradise Road,
Richmond, Surrey TW9 1SR

© Chantelle Shaw 2007

ISBN: 978 0 263 20045 4

Set in Times Roman 16½ on 18½ pt.
16-0508-55229

Printed and bound in Great Britain
by Antony Rowe Ltd, Chippenham, Wiltshire

CHAPTER ONE

ZACHARIE DEVERELL swept along the hospital corridor, paused briefly to check the name above the door before he entered a ward and strode purposefully towards the nurse seated behind the reception desk.

'I'm here to see Freya Addison. I understand she was admitted yesterday,' he added, the hint of impatience in his voice making his accent seem more pronounced. The nurse gaped at him but Zac was used to being stared at. Women had stared at him since he was a teenager and at thirty-five his stunning looks, combined with an aura of wealth and power, meant that he was accustomed to being the centre of attention.

When it suited him he would respond to a flirtatious look with one of his devastating smiles, but today he had other things on his mind. There was only one reason why he was here, he acknowledged grimly, and the sooner he saw Freya and told her exactly what he thought of her latest stunt, the better.

'Um…Miss Addison…' Thoroughly flustered by the presence of six feet four of brooding Frenchman holding an angelic-looking child in his arms, the nurse hurriedly flicked through the pile of papers in front of her. 'Oh, yes, down the corridor, third door on the left—but you can't see her at the moment, the doctor is with her. Please, wait a minute, Mr…?'

The Frenchman was already striding along the corridor and the nurse scooted around the desk and chased after him.

'Deverell,' he murmured coolly, not slowing his steps. 'My name is Zac Deverell and it is imperative that I see Miss Addison immediately.'

Freya sat on her hospital bed and stared gloomily at her bandaged wrist. The past twenty-four hours had been hellish and she hoped that any minute now she would wake up and find that it had all been a nightmare. Instead the throbbing ache of her badly sprained wrist and a splitting headache were evidence of the force with which her car had ploughed into a fallen tree, brought down during the ferocious storm that had hit the south coast.

She had been on her way home from the yacht club where she worked as a receptionist and fortunately hadn't yet collected her little daughter from the day nursery when the accident had happened. Aimee was safe, and she was lucky to be alive, she acknowledged with a shudder, but her car was damaged beyond repair and she was going to have to take time off work, which was not going to help her ailing finances.

She had spent the night in the hospital with mild concussion and the doctor had explained that the ligaments in her wrist had been torn and she would need to wear a support bandage for several weeks. After prescribing strong painkillers he had told her she could go home, but she was worried about how she was going to manage to carry Aimee and her pushchair up and down the four flights of stairs to their attic flat when she only had the use of one hand.

She would have to ask her grandmother for help, she fretted, her thoughts turning to the woman who had brought her up after her mother had abandoned her when she was a baby. But Joyce Addison had taken on the role of parent out of a sense of duty rather than affection. Freya had endured a loveless childhood and when she had fallen pregnant and immediately been dumped by her baby's father, her grandmother had made it clear that she would not support her or her child.

She guessed Joyce had been furious when the hospital contacted her yesterday and passed on her request that she should collect Aimee from nursery. She had half expected her grandmother to turn up at the hospital last night with the toddler in tow, but there had been no word from the older woman and Freya was growing increasingly anxious. She glanced up expectantly when the door opened and felt a sharp pang of disappointment when a nurse entered the small side ward.

'Have you heard anything from my grandmother? Has she phoned? She's looking after my daughter but she's due to fly to New York any day now.'

'As far as I know, there has been no word from your grandmother, but your daughter is here at the hospital,' the nurse said cheerfully. 'Her uncle's looking after her. I'll tell him he can come in.'

'Uncle?' Freya stared at the nurse in bewilderment. Aimee didn't have an *uncle*.

'Yes, I asked Mr Deverell to wait in the visitor's lounge while the doctor was with you, but I know he's impatient to see you,' the nurse added wryly. The Frenchman had to be the sexiest male on the planet, but it had been evident from the haughty expression in his flashing blue eyes that patience wasn't one of his strong points.

The nurse disappeared before Freya could question her further. The world had gone mad, she decided as she ran a shaky hand through her hair. The name Deverell conjured up a face from the past that she had spent the past two years desperately trying to forget and hearing it again caused a peculiar cramping sensation in the pit of her stomach. The nurse must have made a mistake. But who was this mysterious uncle—who exactly was looking after Aimee?

'Mum-mum!'

She glanced towards the door at the sound of her daughter's gurgling laughter and focused on Aimee's cherubic face, a heady mixture of love and relief coursing through her veins. But almost instantly her gaze moved higher and clashed with the cool blue stare of the man who had haunted her dreams for the past two years.

'Zac?' she whispered disbelievingly.

Zac Deverell; billionaire businessman, renowned playboy and chief executive of the globally successful company Deverell's, which owned exclusive department stores around the world, instantly seemed to dominate the room. He was even more gorgeous than she remembered, she thought numbly as her brain struggled to assimilate the shocking reality of his presence at the end of her bed. He was tall, lean and devastatingly good-looking, his black jeans and matching sweater were effortlessly stylish and accentuated his athletic build.

Weakly Freya closed her eyes. For a few

seconds the image of his bronzed, muscular torso and the covering of fine black hairs that arrowed down over his flat stomach flooded her mind. Zac was the epitome of male perfection. For a few brief, incredible months she'd enjoyed free access to his body and had revelled in the feel of his satiny skin beneath her fingertips as she'd trailed a daring path over the solid strength of his thighs. She had a vivid recall of how it had felt to lie beneath him, skin on skin, their limbs entwined so that two became one…

With a low murmur she released her breath and stared at his face, noting the male beauty of his sharp cheekbones and square chin, and the way a lock of his jet-black hair had fallen over his brow. His eyes were the deep, dense blue of a Mediterranean summer sky—the same shade as Aimee's eyes. The thought sent her crashing back to reality and she frowned at the way her daughter was sitting contentedly in his arms. It was a sight she had dreamed of frequently, but never in her wildest fantasies had she expected it to happen.

'What are *you* doing here? And since when did

you become Aimee's uncle?' Shock seemed to have robbed her of her strength and to her chagrin her voice sounded pathetically weak.

Zac regarded her silently for a moment, his black brows drawn together in a harsh frown. 'It was easier to tell the hospital staff that I'm a relative—or would you rather I'd explained that I'm the man you tried to trick into believing was the father of your child?' he queried pleasantly, aware that any hint of aggression in his tone could frighten the little girl sitting on his hip.

Freya gave a bitter laugh. 'It was no trick, *Zac*—Aimee is your daughter.'

'The *hell* she is!' The denial came out as a low hiss and Zac abruptly lowered Aimee onto the bed. He smiled reassuringly at the toddler, making a Herculean effort to mask his impatience from her. It wasn't the child's fault, he reminded himself. With her halo of golden curls and enormous blue eyes, Aimee was angelic. It was her mother who was a cheat and a liar and if Freya hadn't looked so damned fragile he'd be tempted to throttle her for manipulating him into this situation.

'We went through this two years ago, Freya, when you sprang the news that you were pregnant. My response is the same now as it was then,' he told her coldly. 'You might have convinced your grandmother of my paternity but you and I both know you weren't telling the truth—don't we?'

'I've never lied to you,' Freya snapped, stung by the contempt in Zac's eyes. It was the same expression that she'd seen when she'd told him she was expecting his baby—contemptuous disbelief, followed by his devastating accusation that she had obviously cheated on him. The pain in her heart was no less intense, despite the passing of time. In a strange way it was worse. The mental wounds Zac had inflicted on her were far more painful than her injuries. Seeing him again had re-ignited her agony and she wished he would go, before she suffered the ultimate humiliation of breaking down in front of him.

'I no longer care what you think,' she told him wearily, unable to stifle a groan when Aimee scrambled over her and knocked against her sore ribs—bruised in the accident by the force of her seat belt locking against her. 'I can't imagine what you're doing here, but I think it's best if you leave.'

'Believe me, I'm not here through choice,' Zac ground out savagely. 'I was at Deverell's London office this morning to give a press conference announcing record profits made by the Oxford Street store, when your grandmother turned up with your daughter. Presumably you'd planned the timing of her visit to create maximum impact,' he added harshly. 'Her accusation, that Aimee is my child, was overheard by several journalists as well as members of my staff and rumours have already got back to the Deverell board.'

'Aimee was in *London?* I don't understand,' Freya said sharply, frowning in confusion. 'The hospital phoned my grandmother yesterday and asked her to look after Aimee. Where is Nana Joyce now?'

'Jetting off across the Atlantic for the start of her cruise, I imagine,' Zac replied. 'She went on about how she'd saved for years for a round-the-world trip and that nothing, not even the fact that you were in hospital, would induce her to miss it.'

His eyes darkened as he remembered his meeting with Joyce Addison.

'I'm sick to death of feckless fathers,' she told him when she marched into his office wheeling a pushchair in front of her and handed him an enormous holdall, which, she informed him, contained all the necessary paraphernalia for an eighteen-month-old child. 'I was left to bring up Freya after her mother got herself pregnant at sixteen by some shiftless Lothario she'd met at a funfair. Sadie soon got bored of motherhood and went off, leaving me stuck with a child I didn't want.

'I thought I'd warned Freya of the dangers of handsome men who want nothing more than a good time,' Joyce continued, trailing her eyes over him as if he were some sort of *stud,* Zac recalled furiously. 'I told her when you offered her a job on that fancy boat of yours that you were only after one thing, and evidently you both got more than you bargained for. But now it's time you took responsibility for your actions.

'I don't know how long Freya is going to be in hospital and I'm not waiting to find out. If you won't look after Aimee, you'd better hand her over to social services, because I refuse to be landed with another baby.'

Joyce Addison's vitriolic tirade had captured the attention of everyone at the Deverell offices—although his staff had done their best to hide their curiosity, Zac conceded darkly. The whole, unbelievable scenario had been *bloody* humiliating, he thought bitterly—and there was only one person he could blame.

'You can drop the act, Freya,' he said coldly. 'It's quite obvious you told your grandmother to bring Aimee to me, and, having met Joyce, I can't even blame you,' he went on, ignoring Freya's gasp. 'I wouldn't leave a dog in your grandmother's care, let alone a young child. But if all this is a ploy to get money out of me in the form of maintenance—you can forget it.'

He glared at her, his anger increasing when he felt his body's response to Freya, with her small, heart-shaped face and mass of silky honey-blonde hair. She had intrigued him for barely three months, but two years on he could instantly recall her slender, pale limbs and small, firm breasts. The passion they had shared had been explosive, he acknowledged, aware of an uncomfortable tightening in his groin as unbidden memories surfaced. He had wanted her from the moment she'd first joined the crew of his luxury yacht, *The Isis,* and the attraction between them had been mutual.

Shy, innocent Freya had been unable to hide her awareness of him and he had wasted no time persuading her into his bed. Although it had been a shock to discover just how innocent she was, he thought grimly. He liked his women to be self-confident and experienced in bed—willing participants in the mutual exchange of sexual pleasure without the pressure of emotional ties. But the temptation of her satiny skin as she curled her legs around him and the enticement of her breathless whispers begging him to make love to her had been impossible to resist. She had proved a willing pupil and he had delighted in tutoring her. Her shyness and inexperience had been refreshing and against his better judgement he had invited her to move into his penthouse apartment as his mistress.

It was a decision he had later regretted and after discovering her to have slept with another man behind his back he had evicted her from his life with ruthless efficiency. His bed had not remained empty for very long. His vast fortune meant that there would always be a queue of willing candidates vying to be his mistress, he acknowledged cynically.

He had hardly given Freya a thought since he'd dismissed her back to England and it irritated him to realise that the chemistry between them still burned as fiercely as ever.

'I did not instruct my grandmother to bring Aimee to you,' Freya said shakily, still struggling to accept that Zac was really standing in front of her. 'Trust me; you're the *last* person I'd ever turn to for help.' She glared at him, her green eyes blazing with anger and unconcealed hurt. He was so beautiful, she thought painfully. She couldn't tear her eyes from him and the sight of his broad chest and powerful abdominal muscles, delineated by his close-fitting, fine-knit jumper, made her insides melt.

Zac was utterly gorgeous but fatally flawed,

she reminded herself. His arrogance and cynicism had almost destroyed her, but her body seemed to have a short memory and was responding to his closeness with humiliating eagerness. He had treated her *diabolically*. When she had needed him most, he had let her down and demolished her pride with his foul accusations that she had been a two-timing whore. Two years ago he'd made it clear that she meant nothing to him, so why was her heart racing? And why was her brain intent on recalling every detail of his kiss, the feel of his hands on her body…?

Frantically she dragged her mind from her memories. 'I admit I once told Nana Joyce that you're Aimee's father—she kept on and on about it, and it's the truth, whatever you might think,' she stated with quiet dignity. 'You were the first and only man I've ever slept with, Zac,' she whispered sadly, 'but you had your own reasons for choosing not to believe me, didn't you?'

Zac's expression of cool disinterest did not flicker and his only reaction to her last statement was a slight quirk of his brows. 'And what was that, *chérie*?'

'You'd decided *before* I told you I was pregnant that you wanted to end our relationship. After three months together you'd grown tired of me. Don't deny it,' she said fiercely. 'I recognised the signs, the way you mentally withdrew from me during those last few weeks that we were together. The only time we were close was in bed, and even then you were…distant.'

'Not that distant,' Zac replied mockingly. 'Your voracious appetite for sex wouldn't allow any distance between us, would it, Freya? I still find it amazing that you had the energy to sleep with anyone else when you put so much effort into sleeping with me.'

His deliberate cruelty skewered Freya's heart and she blinked back the rush of tears that burned her eyelids. 'How dare you?' she whispered thickly. 'Don't try and appease your guilty conscience by blaming me. You wanted rid of me because you'd set your sights on Annalise Dubois. You were determined to make her your next mistress, but an ex who was pregnant with your baby would have seriously cramped your style.'

In her agitation she leapt off the bed and her

head spun. The blood drained from her face and she swayed unsteadily before collapsing back onto the mattress.

'Enough,' Zac growled as he stepped forwards and caught Aimee who was determinedly trying to wriggle off the bed. 'You're upsetting the child.' He set Aimee down on the floor and stared speculatively at her blonde curls for a moment before glancing back at her mother.

'I don't want anything from you,' Freya stated angrily. 'Certainly not money,' she added, unable to hide the flare of contempt in her eyes. 'I just want you to accept that I'm telling the truth.'

She stared into his brilliant blue eyes, that were so like Aimee's, and gave an angry sigh. She had no intention of pursuing him through the courts for a slice of his vast fortune as her grandmother had frequently suggested. He didn't want her and he didn't want Aimee, and that was fine, she'd manage without him. She just wanted him to accept that she had never lied to him. 'Why can't you be honest with me?' she pleaded.

Zac glanced down at her and tensed. Her thin hospital nightgown had come unfastened so that he could see the curve of one small, pale breast. To his utter disgust he felt his body's involuntary reaction—a shaming surge of heat in his loins as desire corkscrewed in his gut.

She'd proved herself to be a faithless whore, damn it, who was still brazenly trying to pass off another man's child as his. It was humiliating to realise the effect she still had on him. He didn't want to want her; it dented his pride to know that he was seriously tempted to wind his hand into her hair, angle her head and plunder the softness of her moist pink lips in a kiss that would remind her of the passion they had once shared.

Instead he forced himself to move away from the bed and stared out of the window at the rain lashing against the pane. 'What would you know of honesty, Freya?' he demanded coldly, his facial muscles tightening so that his skin was stretched taut over his cheekbones. 'Did you really think I wouldn't find out about your secret assignations with that anaemic-looking street artist Simon Brooks?

'Monaco is a small place and gossip runs rife. I am—' he shrugged his shoulders in a typically

Gallic gesture '—well known in the principality and the speculation that I was being cuckolded by my mistress soon reached my ears. I might even have found the situation amusing,' he drawled sardonically. 'It was certainly a novelty. But your attempts to saddle me with another man's child were not so funny, *chérie*.'

'I swear I never slept with Simon,' Freya said urgently. 'The bodyguard you'd assigned to protect me made a mistake that day. But at the time— when you said all those terrible things to me—I couldn't think straight.' She had been so devastated by Zac's refusal to believe that she was carrying his baby and so shocked by his accusation that she had slept with Simon that her mind had gone blank and she had simply walked out of his apartment without even trying to defend herself. 'I've had a long time to think about things since then,' she added bitterly, 'and now I believe I know what happened.' She paused for a moment and stared at Zac, faint hope bubbling in her chest when he remained silent. It was the first time since the fateful night two years ago that they had actually spoken properly. The first time he had listened.

'It's true I spent a lot of time with Simon, but he was my friend, nothing more. You were always busy working and I was lonely,' she admitted quietly, thinking of the young English art student who had befriended her during her stay in Monaco. Simon had been touring the Mediterranean coast, scraping a living selling his paintings. Unlike Zac's glamorous friends, he'd seemed refreshingly ordinary and down to earth, and she had enjoyed his company. 'We weren't lovers—he was just someone from home that I liked to talk to.'

'And I suppose Michel was lying when he told me he'd seen you and Brooks leave the beach arm in arm to return to his camper van?' Zac drawled. '*Sacré bleu!* I paid Michel to protect you, but when he saw your distinctive pink jacket hanging on the van door and glimpsed you and your floppy-haired artist rolling around inside, he didn't know what to do. He certainly didn't want to be seen as a voyeur,' he added, his lip curling in distaste. 'My wealth brings with it a very real threat of kidnap and Michel knew that, as my mistress, you were vulnerable. He didn't want to leave you without protection, but neither did he want to hang around watching your sexual gymnastics with Brooks. In the end he phoned me to ask my advice—while I was hurrying back from a business trip to take you out to dinner,' Zac finished grimly.

'Your announcement as soon as I walked through the door that you were pregnant was ill-timed to say the least, *chérie*,' he continued when it was evident that she was beyond words. 'I'd just learned from a man I trusted implicitly that you and Brooks were lovers, and I was certain that I wasn't the child's father. It wasn't difficult to work out that you were pregnant by your penniless artist and hoping to pass the baby off as mine.'

The cold fury in his eyes caused Freya to shiver but this was possibly the only chance she would ever have to defend herself and make Zac see that he was wrong about her. 'Michel didn't see me,' she insisted desperately. 'He just thought he did. I'd gone to the beach to meet Simon and a group of his friends, including his girlfriend. Kirsten was feeling cold and I lent her my jacket before I walked into the town. She has blonde hair like mine and Michel must have mistaken her for me…' She stumbled to a halt, her heart sinking at the mockery in Zac's eyes. 'I didn't go to Simon's van that day and I was never unfaithful to you, Zac,' she insisted. 'You have to believe me.'

He stared at her in silence for a few moments and then laughed unpleasantly. 'You've had two years to think of a story. Is that really the best you can do, *chérie*?' He paced the room like a caged tiger, his pent up aggression almost tangible. *'Non!'* he stated fiercely, slicing his hand through the air to emphasise his anger. 'I refuse to be manipulated by you. I want a paternity test and once I've proved conclusively that you are a liar, I never want to see you or hear from you again. Do you understand?'

'How can you be so sure that I'm lying?' Freya whispered numbly. Clearly Zac's opinion of her couldn't sink any lower and she was shocked by how much it hurt. The contempt in his tone made her want to shrivel but pride brought her head up. The silence between them vibrated with a tension that shredded her nerves and she visibly flinched when he swung round and stared at her.

His expression filled her with a curious sense of foreboding and she felt her stomach churn. She could not tear her gaze from the sculpted beauty of his face but his eyes were hard and cold and, despite the stifling warmth of the hospital ward, she shivered.

Zac paused and then said unemotionally, 'Because I had a vasectomy—years before we met. The truth is, *chérie*, that it's medically impossible for Aimee to be my daughter.'

CHAPTER TWO

ZAC watched the shock and confusion on Freya's face with clinical detachment before he glanced at Aimee. The little girl stared up at him solemnly, her pretty little face surrounded by her mass of curls and her pink cheeks glowing with health. She was not a Deverell, thank God, he thought with quiet certainty. This child would not suffer the way his twin sisters had suffered— victims of the devastating illness that had taken their lives before they were a year old.

He had been a teenager when his mother had given birth to twins. The babies had appeared normal but within a few months both had died from an incurable genetic disorder and after their deaths doctors had warned his parents there was a fifty-per-cent chance that he had also been affected. He had escaped the illness but there was no test available to show if he carried the gene.

The trauma of watching his sisters die and witnessing his parents' grief had never faded. As an adult he had made the decision that he could not risk the slightest chance of passing on the gene to his own children and had taken the necessary steps to ensure that he would never be a father. The faint regret he'd felt at the time had soon faded and he had moved on, determined to enjoy his life and take advantage of the benefits his billion-pound fortune afforded him.

He couldn't have children, but why would he want to be tied down to the responsibilities of a family when he could afford fast cars, power boats and all the trappings of his wealth? He enjoyed an endless supply of beautiful women who entertained him briefly before he grew bored and looked around for new pleasures.

Freya had intrigued him for longer than most but he had never viewed her as becoming a permanent feature in his life. It hadn't occurred to him to mention his vasectomy when she had been his mistress and he felt under no obligation to explain the reason for it now.

Freya stared wildly at Zac, feeling as though the world had actually shifted on its axis. 'The operation must have failed,' she croaked, struggling to assimilate his shocking announcement. 'I don't understand how it could have happened, but Aimee is your child,' she insisted desperately.

'Don't be ridiculous,' Zac snapped irritably. 'It's impossible.' Although that wasn't strictly true, he acknowledged silently. He'd always known that the procedure carried a one-in-two-thousand chance of reversal, but when Freya had sprung the news of her pregnancy, less than an hour after his security guard, Michel, had seen her with Simon Brooks, he had angrily assumed that she'd been having an affair with the Englishman for weeks and that the baby she was carrying couldn't possibly be his own. He was still convinced that this was the case and he felt a surge of disgust for Freya and her pathetic excuses.

He would have marginally more respect for her if she stopped lying and admitted that she'd been caught out, he brooded darkly, his lip curling in contempt. She was beautiful—more so, if anything, than she had been two years ago—but beneath her exquisite shell she was rotten to the core and once he had the proof he would have nothing more to do with her.

'The nurse informed me that you've been discharged,' he said tersely, raking his eyes over Freya's pale face as he strode towards the door. 'Hurry up and get dressed. We're flying to Monaco immediately where I'll make the necessary arrangements to carry out the DNA test and end this wild speculation once and for all.'

Half an hour later, Freya's temper was at boiling point. Zac seemed to think he could just waltz back into her life and take over. 'I am *not* going to Monaco with you,' she repeated for the twentieth time as she followed him across the hospital car park and watched him strap Aimee into the child-seat that his secretary had apparently lent him when he'd driven down from London. It was still raining hard and he had turned up the collar of his leather jacket. With his hair slicked back from his face and his black brows lowered in an ominous scowl he looked more gorgeous than ever and she groaned silently at her body's traitorous response to him.

He was mean, moody and magnificent, she thought bleakly, not to mention the most arrogant, overbearing man she had ever met. Two years ago he had swept her away on his boat and straight into his bed. She had given him her virginity but he had stolen her heart, she thought sadly. After a lifetime devoid of any emotional security she had willingly become his mistress, but his cruel rejection had almost destroyed her and she could not risk returning to the place where she had once been so happy.

'I agree that we need to do a paternity test,' she said when he made no reply. 'But why can't we do it here in England? I don't want to go anywhere with you.'

'Tough.' Zac checked Aimee was secure and then opened the driver's door and slid into the car. 'I have an urgent meeting with the Deverell board tomorrow at the Monaco office and so it's more convenient for me to have it done in my private clinic at home. Get in the car,' he snapped testily when she continued to stand outside in the rain. 'I've chartered a private jet and my pilot can't wait all day.'

Freya glowered at him as she climbed reluctantly into the passenger seat. Her heart was thumping painfully in her chest and she wished she had the nerve to snatch Aimee and run. The torrential rain, her injured wrist and the bitter knowledge that he could effortlessly outmatch her in speed and strength made her stay put, but she edged as far away as possible from him once inside the car and stared pointedly out of the window.

'You'll have to give me directions to your flat,' he said when he turned out of the hospital gates. 'Aimee's pushchair and a bag of her clothes are in the boot, courtesy of your grandmother,' he added, his voice simmering with barely concealed anger. 'You can have twenty minutes to pack, but I intend to leave within the next hour.'

Freya leaned back and closed her eyes wearily, overwhelmed by his determination. When Zac wanted his own way he invariably got it—but unless he intended to kidnap her and Aimee, he couldn't make them get on his plane.

She was acutely conscious of him sitting beside her and when she peeped at him from beneath her lashes, the sight of his strong, tanned hands on the wheel made her feel weaker than ever. Once those hands had skimmed every inch of her body and explored her so intimately that the memory made her blush. He smelled of rain and damp leather, and the subtle scent of the cologne he favoured was achingly familiar, tantalising her senses and forcing her to remember the mind-blowing passion they had once shared.

It was over, she reminded herself angrily as she tore her gaze from his stern profile. He had tried and convicted her before she'd even understood the crime she was supposed to have committed. In a strange way his revelation about his vasectomy was almost a relief. His savage anger and rejection two years ago had destroyed her, but now at least she could understand why he had been so ready to believe that she'd been having an affair with Simon.

The fact that he had never mentioned his vasectomy when she'd lived with him emphasised how little she'd meant to him. The question of children had never arisen because she'd been Zac's mistress and he hadn't wanted a permanent relationship with her.

But the operation must have reversed. She didn't know much about the procedure but presumably it hadn't worked properly because Aimee was undoubtedly his daughter, she thought on a wave of near hysteria. What other explanation could there be?

After Aimee was born she had briefly considered asking Zac for a DNA test, but had decided against it. His reaction to her pregnancy had shown that he abhorred the idea of fatherhood and she had feared he would only take a reluctant role in his daughter's upbringing.

At eighteen months old, Aimee was a happy, loving child whose confidence was built on the instinctive knowledge that she was loved unconditionally. She would not allow Zac to destroy that confidence, Freya thought fiercely, and she would do everything in her power to ensure that her child grew up with a sense of self-worth that she herself had been denied.

But now Zac had his own reasons for insisting

on a paternity test. He was convinced that the results would absolve him of any responsibility for Aimee and she feared his reaction when he was finally forced to accept the truth.

After fifteen minutes, during which Zac barely contained his frustration as they crawled through the traffic, he pulled up outside the house where Freya occupied the top-floor flat and frowned at the peeling paintwork and general air of decay. 'You live here? *Mon Dieu*, I assume it's in better condition inside.'

'Don't bank on it,' she muttered, feeling a peculiar pain around her heart as she watched Aimee raise her arms for Zac to lift her out of her seat. The little girl was usually shy with strangers. Did she feel a subconscious bond with her father? Freya wondered as she led the way up the front path. Once inside she preceded him up the stairs, aware that his silence was growing more ominous by the minute.

'How were you planning to carry Aimee up and down four flights of stairs with your injured wrist?' he enquired when they finally reached her front door. 'What would you do if there was a fire? You'd never be able to evacuate quickly.'

'I'd manage somehow, just as I always have,' she replied stiffly, hovering in the narrow hallway in a vain attempt to block his way. She didn't want him here, intruding on her life, but he ignored her and stepped past her into the cramped bedsit.

The flat was a mess—it seemed a lifetime ago that she had flown out of the door to drop Aimee at the nursery and continue on to work. Yesterday's breakfast dishes were still piled up in the sink and the clothes-rack was festooned with a selection of her underwear. Zac was glancing around the room with a faint air of disbelief and she wished he would go away. She hated him seeing how she lived. 'It's not ideal, I admit,' she mumbled, 'but it's all I can afford.'

'I can't believe you're bringing a child up here,' Zac said grimly, genuinely shocked by the squalid flat. Freya had obviously done her best to make the place feel homely with brightly coloured cushions scattered on the sofa and Aimee's collection of teddies arranged on the dresser. But nothing could disguise the musty smell of damp plaster, and the bucket strategically placed to catch the rain leaking through the ceiling provided stark evidence that the old house was in a bad state of repair.

Her living conditions were none of his business, he reminded himself as he set Aimee down and she trotted over to her toy box. But now at least he could understand why she was so adamant that he was Aimee's father—perhaps she had genuinely deluded herself into believing it in the hope that he would provide for her child?

Freya shrugged listlessly. 'My living conditions have never bothered you before, Zac. Why the sudden concern?' she asked coolly. She shrugged out of her wet jacket and belatedly remembered that she'd been unable to put on her bra when she had struggled into her clothes at the hospital. Zac's eyes moved over her and to her horror she felt her breasts tighten.

The atmosphere in her tiny flat changed imperceptibly and she was aware of his sudden tension as she hastily folded her arms across her chest to hide the prominent peaks of her nipples. Now was not a good time to remember the connection they had once shared. She tore her gaze from the sensual curve of his mouth and tried to banish the memory of how it had felt when he had crushed her lips beneath his own.

'I meant what I said earlier—I'm not coming to Monaco with you,' she told him firmly, feeling more confident on her home territory. 'You can't make me, unless you intend to bind and gag me and bundle me onto your plane,' she added when he said nothing and simply stared at her as if he could read the thoughts whirling around in her head.

He seemed to dominate the small room and she swallowed when he strolled towards her. 'It's tempting,' he drawled, his blue eyes glinting dangerously. 'Don't goad me, *chérie*, or I might think you are trying to anger me on purpose.'

'Why would I do that?' Freya demanded, despising herself for the way her nerve endings sprang into urgent life at his closeness.

'We always had the most amazing sex after an argument,' he replied silkily, the sudden flare of amusement in his eyes warning her that he was aware of the effect he had on her. Freya blushed furiously and itched to slap him.

'I don't remember sex between us being anything more than mediocre,' she lied. 'Perhaps you're thinking of one of your other lovers Zac. You've had plenty, after all.'

She almost jumped out of her skin when his hand suddenly shot out and he caught hold of her chin, tilting her head so that she had no option but to meet his gaze. 'Nothing about our relationship in the bedroom was mediocre, *chérie*, and if we had more time I'd be tempted to prove that fact.' The flare of heat in his eyes scorched her skin and she focused helplessly on his mouth, her tongue darting out to trace the curve of her bottom lip in an unconscious invitation. The atmosphere was electric, she could almost feel the sparks shooting between them, but then he abruptly released her and moved away, his expression unfathomable.

'Be thankful that I am in a hurry to get back for a dinner date tonight,' he growled as he scooped her underwear from the clothes rack and dumped the pile of pretty lace knickers in her hands. 'And hurry up and pack or you'll find yourself travelling to Monaco *sans* your lingerie.'

Freya glared at him, her jaw aching with the effort of holding back her furious retort. He was so smug, and, as usual, so in control of the situation, nothing ever dented his supreme self-confidence. She hated him for every foul accusation he'd flung at her, every scathing insult that she was an unfaithful, gold-digging tramp. But even though he was looking at her as if she were something unpleasant that had crawled from beneath a stone, she could not deny the inexorable tug of desire that coiled low in her stomach.

It was devastating to realise that, despite everything he had done to her, she still wanted him. Where was her pride? she asked herself. Zac had used her body for sex and abused her fragile heart with his cruelty and contempt. But seeing him again had opened up the feelings she had tried so hard to suppress since he had ruthlessly dismissed her from his life.

She had never got over him, she acknowledged dismally. He had been the love of her life, but the molten heat surging through her veins was caused by lust, not love, she assured herself frantically. She'd learned the hard way never to waste her emotions on him because he had certainly never loved her and he never would.

The last thing she wanted to do was go to Monaco with him, but what choice did she have? she brooded as her gaze fell on her little daughter. As usual, Zac was right; she was never going to manage the stairs with Aimee and the pushchair while her wrist was so painful, and she had lain awake for most of the previous night worrying about how she would cope.

Her heart jolted in her chest as she accepted the unpalatable truth that she would have to go with him for now. She had no idea how long it would take for Zac to arrange a paternity test and await the results but it couldn't be more than a week or two, she consoled herself. And by then her wrist would be stronger and she would be able to return home.

She would go to Monaco, but this time she would be on her guard and would not give in to the undeniable sexual attraction that still smouldered between them, she vowed fiercely. She was no longer a naïve girl, she was an independent woman, and she would not be tempted by the sizzling sexual promise in Zac's bold gaze.

The bright lights of Monaco blazed against a backdrop of black velvet. As the helicopter swooped low over the coastline Zac glanced over his shoulder. Aimee was fast asleep, sitting next to the nanny he had hired. 'We're almost there,' he murmured reassuringly to the uniformed woman. 'May I say how grateful I am that you were able to join us at such short notice, Mrs Lewis.'

Jean Lewis smiled. 'I'm glad to help. With any luck I'll be able to put Aimee straight to bed without waking her. She's worn out, poor poppet.'

With a brief nod, Zac turned back and glanced at Freya who was sitting stiffly beside him, the mutinous tilt of her chin causing him to curse irritably beneath his breath. If anyone had told him when he'd set out for Deverell's London offices that he would return to Monaco with his ex-mistress and her child in tow, he would have laughed out loud, he thought with a humourless smile.

His eyes trailed over her and he felt his body's

involuntary reaction to the sight of her small breasts outlined beneath her blouse. Once again Freya had turned his life upside down. After their bitter parting two years ago, he had neither wanted nor expected to see her again, but, even knowing what she had done, he was finding it impossible to ignore her.

Freya felt Zac's eyes on her and stiffened when he shifted slightly in his seat so that his thigh brushed against hers. When they had left England aboard the private jet, he had sat at the front of the plane, his attention focused exclusively on his laptop. It had suited her fine—she had nothing to say to him that wouldn't blister his ears anyway—but when they'd arrived in Nice and boarded his helicopter for the short journey to Monaco, her heart had sunk when he had sat down next to her.

She had tried her best to ignore him but unfortunately her senses refused to fall into line and she was agonisingly aware of his closeness. The subtle tang of his cologne was tantalisingly familiar, causing her nerve endings to prickle.

She did *not* want to feel like this, she thought

angrily as she edged away from him. It was humiliating to realise that he could still affect her so strongly, despite everything he had done to her. But it had always been the same; she had never been able to resist him and unfortunately just about every other woman on the planet shared her fascination.

The months she had spent with him had been the happiest but also the most nerve-racking of her life and her ever-present fear that he would tire of her had added to her deep insecurity.

Zac was one of Monaco's most eligible bachelors and at the many parties they had attended he had always been the centre of attention. Women had flocked around him and made their interest clear with a bold smile or knowing glance loaded with sensual invitation. He had responded to their blatant flirting with one of his cool, faintly sardonic smiles, and she'd felt reassured. But Annalise Dubois had been different.

The stunning glamour model had pursued Zac with relentless determination and had shamelessly flaunted her spectacular figure in clingy silks and satins that made the most of her eye-catching cleavage.

Beside her, Freya had felt pale and insipid and she hadn't been able to help but notice the way Zac's eyes had lingered appreciatively on the Frenchwoman's curves. Jealousy had been a green-eyed monster that festered in her soul, making her edgy and paranoid. She'd hated to be apart from him and had questioned his every move—every late night at the office or business trip that had taken him away for days at a time.

She'd known that her behaviour had angered him, but as he'd grown increasingly distant from her, so her terror had increased that he had been tiring of her. The only time she had felt secure was when they had been in bed. There at least his passion for her had shown no sign of diminishing, but he had shut her out of every other aspect of his life and she'd felt as though her only role had been to provide convenient sex on demand.

Choking back a cry, she dragged her mind from the past. She had spent the past two years determinedly trying to forget the life she'd shared with Zac and she must be mad to have agreed to return to Monaco with him.

'Do you still live at the penthouse?' she asked stiffly, seizing on the faint hope that he had moved from the elegant, marble-floored apartment where she had once kidded herself that he might fall in love with her.

'*Oui.* The location suits me and I enjoy the view over the harbour,' he replied coolly.

Freya recalled the spectacular view from the penthouse over Monaco's busy port and the vast stretch of the Mediterranean beyond. 'Do you still keep *The Isis* moored there?'

Zac nodded. 'Unfortunately I don't get to spend as much time on her as I'd like. Deverell's is expanding and we're opening several outlets around the world, including the new store in Mayfair. If your grandmother had picked any other day, I would not have been in London,' he added tersely.

His frown told her that he was cursing his bad luck to have been in London on the same day that Joyce Addison had arrived with Aimee, but Freya shuddered to think what would have happened if he hadn't been there.

'I'm glad Nana Joyce found you,' she admitted quietly, forgetting for a moment that they were enemies. 'I don't know what would have happened to Aimee otherwise.'

'Your grandmother would have cared for her, surely?'

Freya's face twisted. 'I don't know. When she found out that I was going to be an unmarried mother, she was adamant that she would have nothing to do with me or my baby. She bitterly resented having to bring me up and when I was a child I lived with foster parents for a while,' she confided dully. 'My mother had married and was moving to South Africa and my grandmother assumed she would take me with her. They had a furious argument when it turned out that I wasn't included in Sadie's new life.'

Zac's mouth tightened and he was aware of a faint tug of compassion. No wonder Freya's self-esteem was non-existent when she had been so cruelly rejected by her own mother. 'Is that when you were put into care?'

Freya nodded. 'I think my grandmother believed that once social services were involved,

Sadie would finally take responsibility for me—but instead she flew out to Durban without even saying goodbye.' Now that she was a mother herself she found it impossible to understand how her own mother had been able to abandon her so easily. It was obvious that Sadie had never loved her, she acknowledged bleakly, but even after all this time, it still hurt.

'After about six months I went back to live with my grandmother…but I was always afraid that she would send me away again and I tried my hardest not to annoy her.' She thought of the years she'd spent skirting around her grandmother like a timid mouse, desperate not to bring attention to herself and pathetically grateful that Nana Joyce allowed her to live with her. It had been a dismal childhood and she was determined that her daughter would never feel so worthless or unloved.

She jerked her head round and stared at Zac. 'I love Aimee more than anything and I won't allow anyone to hurt her. I agree we should do a paternity test—it's time to set the record straight. I just hope you're prepared for the result.'

The fierceness of her tone shook Zac more than he cared to admit, but he immediately dismissed his doubts. She was bluffing, he reassured himself; or else her desperate financial situation had deluded her into believing he was Aimee's father. Either way, he was not going to be drawn into believing her lies.

'I'm prepared for the test results to confirm that you're a common tramp,' he said aggressively. 'Finally you'll have to accept the truth and move on with your life, as I intend to move on with mine.' And ignoring her furious gasp, he turned his head and stared into the dark for the remainder of the flight.

CHAPTER THREE

TEN minutes later the helicopter landed on the roof of the penthouse and Zac lifted Aimee into his arms and preceded Jean Lewis down the steps. 'Laurent, were you able to carry out my instructions?' he greeted his butler.

'Everything is as you asked, sir,' the butler replied in his usual unflappable manner. 'The nursery suppliers delivered a cot and other necessary furnishings and equipment, and the dressing room adjoining the fourth bedroom has been prepared for the child's nanny.' If Laurent was surprised by the request to prepare a room for a baby, his tone gave nothing away and his facial expression remained as bland as ever.

'*Bon,*' Zac murmured as he transferred the sleeping child back into the nanny's arms.

'Please escort Madame Lewis to the nursery and ensure she has everything she requires.'

He swung round and walked back to the helicopter just as Freya reached the bottom step. She looked pale and tired and was clearly in pain but she glared at him when he reached her side.

'There was no need for you to hire a nanny. I can look after Aimee perfectly well.'

'How exactly when you only have the use of one arm?' he asked impatiently. 'Jean Lewis has excellent references and she'll take good care of Aimee.'

'Where has she taken her?' Freya demanded. Her whole arm was throbbing and she felt light-headed with pain but she refused to admit it to Zac—any more than she would admit to feeling jealous that Aimee had settled so happily with Jean Lewis. Her steps slowed and a feeling of panic swept over her as she followed him into the penthouse. She didn't want to be here and she didn't want to remember the past, but memories were bombarding her.

Zac travelled by helicopter as routinely as most people used a car and had regularly swept her off to parties and other glittering social functions outside Monaco, often flying along the coast to Cannes or St Tropez. The parties had always been wonderful, glamorous affairs, but Freya had only had eyes for him and even in a crowded room his slumberous stare had tormented her with the unspoken promise of sensual nirvana to follow. The hours until they could make their excuses and leave had been a slow torture and her anticipation had always been at fever pitch by the time they had climbed back on board the helicopter for the return flight.

There had been something incredibly magical about swooping low over the sea and the towering apartment blocks that lined Monaco's crowded coastline, knowing that in a few short minutes they would be home. The sensual gleam beneath Zac's heavy lids would stoke her excitement and as soon as the rotors came to a halt he would scoop her into his arms and race into the penthouse, stripping her with brisk efficiency along the way.

Sometimes they hadn't even made it to the master bedroom, she remembered as heat suffused her body. In his urgency to make love to her he had deposited her on one of the sitting room sofas, and the feel of the cool leather against her skin had added a new dimension to her pleasure when he had pushed her thighs apart and entered her with one powerful thrust. Their hunger for each other had been insatiable, a wild, primitive passion that had known no bounds as he had dispensed with her inhibitions and made love to her with an inventiveness that still brought a tide of colour to her cheeks.

Heart pounding, she forced her mind back to the present and stumbled along the hall after him. Oh, God, what was she thinking? And why had her libido chosen now to make a comeback when she had spent the last two years living like a nun?

Zac opened the door of the guest bedroom and ushered Freya inside. 'Jean has taken Aimee to the nursery,' he explained, his eyes narrowing speculatively on her hot face.

'Nursery?' Her eyebrows shot up as she frantically dragged her mind from her erotic fantasies and forced herself to concentrate on his words. She remembered Zac's chic, minimalist apartment as a confirmed bachelor pad—when on earth had he installed a nursery?

'I instructed my staff to prepare a room for Aimee since you will both be staying here for the time being. I hope it will be suitable,' he added coldly.

'I'm sure it'll be more suitable than a damp bedsit. I hope you haven't gone to too much bother, Zac—Aimee and I won't be here long,' Freya muttered, unable to disguise the sudden bitterness in her voice as she remembered how she had struggled to afford even the most basic baby equipment. With a click of his fingers Zac could provide everything Aimee needed—it was a pity he was two years too late.

His mouth tightened but he simply said, 'Laurent will serve supper in your room and then I suggest you take your painkillers and go to bed. You look like death.'

Terrific, she really needed reminding that she looked a mess, Freya thought grimly, especially when *he* looked so gorgeous. He had removed his leather jacket and she could not help but notice the way his black sweater moulded his muscular chest. He was lean, dark and so beautiful that it hurt her to look at him, she acknowledged as desire swept through her. Zac possessed a raw sexual magnetism, and, although her mind urged caution, her body was responding to him with a reckless disregard for her emotional safety.

She was trembling; not as a result of the cool night air, she realised shamefully, but with an almost desperate longing to slide her fingers beneath his fine-knit sweater and run her hands over his olive-gold skin to feel the faint abrasion of the wiry hairs that covered his chest. The images from the past were stubbornly refusing to disappear and she felt thoroughly hot and bothered as sexual frustration spiralled in the pit of her stomach. Swallowing hard, she tore her eyes from him and stared at the carpet. 'I forgot my toothbrush. You didn't give me enough time to pack properly.'

'All the toiletries you could possibly need are in your bathroom,' Zac informed her, 'and the clothes you left behind two years ago are still in the wardrobe.'

'Really?' The surprising statement brought her head up. 'I thought you would have wasted no time getting rid of them,' she mumbled, remembering how humiliated she had felt when he'd hustled her out of the apartment. Her face burned at the memory but he merely shrugged disinterestedly.

'I didn't keep them because I was anticipating ever taking you back, *chérie*, if that's what you're thinking,' he drawled laconically. 'I'd forgotten they were there, until the maid found them in the back of the cupboard when she was preparing your room.' He glanced at his watch and strode towards the door. 'I'm going out for the evening. Can you manage to get undressed, or do you need me to help you?'

Freya flashed him a look that told him she'd rather accept help from a self-confessed axe murderer. 'I'll be fine, thanks,' she replied in a cool voice that masked the sharp pang of dismay she felt as she wondered whom he was meeting for his dinner date. Undoubtedly the woman would be stunning and sophisticated—his current mistress? Or someone picked from his little black book? she mused sourly as she fought her irrational surge of jealousy. It was no business of hers whom he dated, she reminded herself, but the devil in her head was determined to have the last word. 'Oh, and, Zac,' she murmured as he strolled towards the door, 'I'm glad you hadn't planned on resuming our relationship because I wouldn't come back to you if you paid me a million pounds.'

His eyes narrowed on her angry face and then dropped lower, to the frantic rise and fall of her breasts. 'You're here now,' he reminded her silkily.

'Only because you forced me to come—I don't want to be here.'

'*Non, chérie,* I can see that.' The mockery in his voice taunted her long after he had stepped into the hall and closed her door, and with a yelp of impotent fury Freya spun round and stared at her reflection in the full length mirror. No wonder Zac had looked so smug, she thought dismally as she stared at her flushed face. Her pupils had dilated to the size of saucers and her lips were parted, practically begging for him to kiss her, while the hard peaks of her nipples pushing provocatively against her blouse were shameful evidence that he turned her on. Her body had turned traitor from the moment Zac had arrived at the hospital, and to make her humiliation complete it was clear that he was well aware of the effect he had on her.

Uttering a furious oath at her stupidity, she went to check on Aimee, who was sleeping soundly in one of the guest bedrooms that had now been transformed into a nursery. A temporary nursery, Freya decided firmly. Zac was going to get the shock of his life when he learned that he was Aimee's father, but she was under no illusion that he would welcome the news and she intended to return to England as soon as possible, before Aimee ever realised that he did not love her.

She didn't know what Zac would do after the test result, but she wasn't holding her breath that he would apologise for misjudging her so terribly. At best she guessed he would offer some sort of financial support for his daughter, but she would put the money in trust for when Aimee was older. She did not want a penny of his fortune for herself and once she was over the temporary setback of her injured wrist, which had partly forced her to come to Monaco with him, she hoped she would never have to set eyes on him again.

Soon after she had returned to her room the butler Laurent arrived bearing a light, fluffy omelette for her supper. He was unfailingly polite but gave no indication that he remembered her from when she had lived briefly at the penthouse. Presumably her role as Zac's mistress had been quickly filled, probably by Annalise Dubois, she brooded miserably. Was Zac with Annalise tonight? The thought was enough to ruin her appetite and she toyed with her food before heading for the bathroom where she struggled to shower while keeping her bandaged arm out of the spray. By the time she had finished she felt sick from the pain of her injured wrist and after swallowing a couple of painkillers she crawled into bed, desperate for sleep to swallow her in its comforting folds.

Zac swung his powerful sports car into the underground car park and rode the lift up to the penthouse apartment. Dinner had been an unmitigated disaster, he brooded darkly as he unfastened his tie and shoved it in the pocket of his dinner jacket. Not that it had been Nicole's fault. She had looked stunning tonight and her low-cut dress with its thigh-high split down one side had left little to his imagination.

Throughout the meal in one of Monte Carlo's finest restaurants, she had been on sparkling form and had prattled on endlessly about her life, which seemed to consist of shopping or sunbathing on Daddy's yacht, and in the rare lulls in her conversation her smile had sent the subtle signals indicating her willingness to spend the night with him.

It had been their third date, after all, he mused cynically, and the unspoken rules of the game they were both playing dictated that tonight the attractive brunette had expected their relationship to progress to a full-blown sexual affair. But somewhere between the *entrée* and dessert he had lost his appetite for both the food and his companion, and instead of envisaging Nicole's tanned, lissom limbs his mind had seemed intent on recalling every detail of Freya's slender figure.

He had never known another woman to have

such pale skin. It was as if even the sun's rays had not been permitted to touch her and his hands had been the first to stroke her virginal flesh— as they had, he acknowledged, feeling an uncomfortable tightness in his groin. He had been Freya's first lover and, if he was honest, sex with her had been an amazing experience he had never come close to repeating with any other woman.

And he had tried. He'd never professed to be a monk, he conceded sardonically, but sitting in the restaurant with Nicole tonight he'd realised that he did not feel the slightest desire for her and after driving her home he had politely refused her offer of a nightcap. Clearly disappointed, Nicole had eventually accepted his rejection, but he didn't feel good about it—in fact he felt intensely irritated with himself, life in general, and, at the top of the list, the woman who had managed to disrupt his comfortable existence in less than twenty-four hours.

With a muttered oath he strode into the penthouse and headed for the lounge and the well-stocked bar, but the sight of Freya curled up on the sofa caused him to halt abruptly. The low coffee table in front of her was littered with books and papers and she was leafing through the pages of a thick folder, so engrossed that she seemed to be unaware of him.

For a few seconds Zac stood still and allowed his eyes to roam over her mass of blonde hair and perfectly defined heart-shaped face. Her grey silk robe was vaguely familiar from the past and he frowned as he focused on the way the edges had parted to reveal the wisp of silk and lace beneath.

Every item of clothing he had bought for her when she'd lived with him had been chosen with the express purpose of pleasing him, particularly her nightwear, and his mouth tightened cynically as he wondered whether she had changed into the sexy negligee set deliberately to taunt him. Freya was still absorbed in her books and his ir-ritation upped a notch. Being ignored was a new experience for him and, giving an angry shrug of his shoulders, he stepped into the room.

Only then did she glance up. 'Zac…' She blinked at him and fire surged through his veins when he took in the image of her silky blonde hair framing her flushed face. Her skin was bare of make-up, but

somehow that made her sexier, he decided as he
studied her closely, noting the dusting of freckles
on her nose and the fact that her long eyelashes
were tipped with gold. She was staring up at him
with her wide witch's eyes, casting her magic, and
with a jolt he realised that he suddenly felt more
alive than he had done in months.

'I wasn't expecting you to wait up for me,
chérie,' he drawled as he crossed to the bar and
poured himself a large cognac.

'Don't worry, I wasn't,' she replied shortly. 'I
didn't even know you would come back tonight.'
She'd lain in bed torturing herself with images
of him making love to the woman he had taken
to dinner, until she'd given up hoping she'd fall
asleep and had dug out her college books.

Now she stumbled to her feet and clutched the
front of her robe that seemed intent on parting to
reveal the skimpy excuse for a nightgown under-
neath. In the rush to pack for the trip to Monaco,
she had forgotten several essential items, including the oversized, comfortable tee shirts she
usually wore in bed. The nightwear she had left
behind at the penthouse had been chosen for se-

duction rather than sleep, and she blushed when
Zac raked his eyes over her in open appreciation.

'Now that you are here, it's time I left,' she
mumbled, hastily gathering up her books. In her
desperation to escape him, she dropped her folder
and papers flew everywhere. 'I couldn't sleep, so
I thought I'd catch up on some work,' she babbled
when Zac leaned down to gather up the pages and
his hand briefly brushed against hers.

'What kind of work?' he asked curiously. He
handed her the sheaf of papers and frowned
when she quickly snatched her hand away. 'You
don't have to run away from me, Freya. We may
have been forced together under difficult cir-
cumstances but I'm sure we're both adult enough
to manage a civil conversation.' He straightened
up. 'Can I get you a drink?'

For a moment Freya was tempted to flee, un-
convinced that she could manage any kind of conversation with him. It wasn't as if she'd had much
practice, she thought wryly. Her time as Zac's
mistress had been spent mainly in the bedroom
and they hadn't wasted time on idle chit chat.

But the sight of him had inflamed her senses

and sleep seemed as impossible now as it had two hours ago. Perhaps a drink would help her to relax? 'White wine, please—a small glass.' She hovered awkwardly while Zac poured her drink and mumbled her thanks when he handed her the glass, his terse, 'Sit down,' causing her to sink back into her seat. He sprawled on the opposite sofa, his white silk shirt open at the throat and his ankle balanced across his thigh in a position of indolent ease—lithe, tanned and so stomach-churningly sexy that Freya hastily tore her eyes from him and took a large gulp of wine.

'What job do you do that requires you to sit up working until midnight?' he asked again, his brow furrowing. He was regularly at his desk until the early hours, but he was the chief executive of a global business empire and a self-confessed workaholic.

'It's not my job exactly—I'm doing a home study course for an English degree,' Freya told him. 'One day I hope to train to be a teacher so that my career will fit around Aimee's schooling, but obviously I need to work and can't afford to go to college full-time. The only free time I have to study is at night, when she's in bed.' She didn't add that after a long day at work and the responsibilities of being a single mother, she often had to force herself to pull out her books, which was why she had fallen behind with the work and had several assignment deadlines looming.

Zac hid his flare of surprise. During the months that Freya had lived with him, he had never really got to know her. His workload had been particularly heavy and after a long day at the office he had simply wanted to take her to bed. He had asked about her day out of politeness rather than any real interest and had thanked his lucky stars that she wasn't one of those women who insisted on regaling him with every detail of her life.

He had found her quiet, gentle nature soothing, and, if he was honest, he had missed the calming effect she seemed to have on him after he had thrown her out. But now he realised that he knew very little about her. Perhaps it was her faint air of mystery that intrigued him, he debated as he drained his glass and stretched his arms along the back of the sofa, his eyes skimming over her and lingering on the fall of her silky hair. 'It's obvious from the state of your flat that you're struggling financially. Why don't you receive any support from Brooks?' he demanded curtly. 'Are you no longer in contact with him?'

The wine had been a bad idea, Freya decided as she carefully set her glass down on the coffee-table. It seemed to have gone straight to her head and loosened the constraints that held her anger in check. 'As a matter of fact I do see Simon occasionally,' she said with deliberate calm. 'We've remained friends, despite the fact that he now lives in Italy. I'm sure he would help me out if I asked him, but Aimee isn't his child and there's no reason for him to support her. That responsibility lies with her father, wouldn't you say?' She glared at him across the coffee-table, twin spots of colour flaring on her cheeks, but Zac held her gaze, his bland expression giving no clue to his thoughts.

'Absolutely—and I hope you find him, *chérie*,' he murmured. He raised his glass. 'What shall we drink to—absent fathers?' Beneath the mockery Freya caught the anger in his voice and indignation surged through her. What right did he have to be angry? She was the one who struggled to combine being a single mother with the necessity to work and pay the bills. He lived here in his penthouse apartment enjoying a life of unimaginable luxury, with no understanding of the real world or how many times she had felt overwhelmed by her responsibilities.

But voicing her resentment would get her nowhere. Zac was convinced that Aimee wasn't his child and, in fairness, she could understand why. But the very fact that he'd had a vasectomy meant that he did not want to be a father and his present anger was going to be nothing compared with his fury when he learned the truth.

'I guess we'll just have to wait for the results of the paternity test,' she muttered as she got to her feet. Suddenly she was bone-weary and could scarcely believe it had only been twelve hours ago that Zac had stormed into the hospital and back into her life. Returning to the penthouse and reliving the memories of the life she had shared with him was more agonising than she had anticipated and she felt the sting of tears behind her eyelids. 'I wish I hadn't come here,' she flung at him angrily. 'Aimee and I could have stayed in a hotel instead of being here with you and your horrible, suspicious mind.'

Black brows winged upwards at her outburst. 'I've already explained that I'd like the reason for your visit to Monaco to remain a private affair and I prefer to keep you here under my control. I've arranged for a nurse from the clinic to visit tomorrow to take the necessary mouth swabs,' he informed her coolly. He drained his glass and stood up, instantly dwarfing her. He was too much for her to cope with when her emotions were so precariously balanced, but when she moved to step past him, he blocked her path. 'The results should be back within ten days, and then you'll be free to leave. Until then I'm afraid we're stuck with each other. But it's possible we'll find some compensation in being forced to spend time in each other's company.'

Freya gave a disbelieving laugh. 'Such as?'

Too late she recognised the gleam in his eyes and her heart lurched as his arm shot out and snaked around her waist.

'Such as this,' he said, ignoring her punitive

struggles to escape from his grip as he lowered his mouth with slow deliberation until it hovered millimetres above hers. 'You may dislike me almost as much as I dislike you, but unfortunately sexual desire seems to have no respect for our mutual loathing—does it, Freya?'

Before she could formulate a reply, he closed the gap between their mouths and kissed her, his lips moving over hers in a fierce assault that demanded her response. The mockery of his last statement rang in her ears and she pressed her lips together in a desperate attempt to deny him. How could he kiss her like this if he hated her? her brain asked numbly, but it was clear that her body did not care. It had been so long since she had been in his arms and she had missed him so much.

Weakly she tried to push against his chest but her senses flared at the scent of his cologne and the male heat emanating from him and slowly her fingers uncurled and crept up to his shoulders. His tongue probed relentlessly against her mouth until, with a little gasp, she parted her lips and he instantly thrust between them while his hand tangled in her hair and he angled her head to his satisfaction.

'Zac…' he dealt with her mumbled protest with swift efficiency, deepening the kiss until it was flagrantly possessive, his lips branding her tender flesh as his hunger escalated and he sought her total capitulation. Only when he felt her tentative response, felt the soft stroke of her tongue inside his mouth, did he ease the pressure a little as he explored her with an erotic intent that left her trembling and breathless, and with a moan of despair Freya curled her hands around his neck and clung to him shamelessly.

A quiver ran through her when she felt his hand slide up and down her body, curve possessively around her buttocks and then move up to her waist. With a deft movement he loosened the belt of her robe and pushed the material aside to reveal the wisp of lace beneath that did little to hide her breasts from his hungry gaze. His eyes darkened and with slow deliberation he pushed the strap of her nightdress over her shoulder, lower and lower until one breast was completely bared.

'No…' she whispered frantically, knowing that she should stop him but desperate to feel his hands on her sensitive flesh. She'd been starved of him for so long and she whimpered when he cupped the soft mound with his lean brown fingers and flicked his thumb pad back and forth over the taut peak of her nipple. Liquid heat coursed through her and she moaned softly and leaned into him, but he tensed and abruptly lifted his head.

'You were always completely uninhibited in the bedroom,' he stated harshly, staring down at her with undisguised contempt in his eyes. 'Don't look at me with those doe eyes and tell me you don't want to be here because I know perfectly well what you want, *chérie*, and I think I've demonstrated rather conclusively that I can provide it.'

The note of self-disgust in his voice destroyed Freya even more than his deliberate cruelty. Clearly Zac had been surprised by his desire for her and shocked by the level of his need, but he *despised* himself for it almost as much as he despised her. When he released her she swayed unsteadily and for one horrific moment she actually thought she was going to be sick.

'There's little point in denying that you can still push all the right buttons,' she said bitterly, colour storming into her pale cheeks when she remembered her wanton response to him. 'But it's just lust, Zac. I'm a normal woman and I have the usual needs, which I have no intention of indulging,' she added on a note of fierce pride. 'Don't get it into your head that it's anything more than that. You don't mean anything to me.'

She left her books on the table and flew across to the door, desperate to reach the relative sanctuary of her room, but his confident drawl followed her.

'I'm glad to hear it, *chérie*, because when I choose to take you to bed it will be on the strict understanding that your body is the only thing I desire—your conniving little mind I can do without. *Bonne nuit*,' he murmured silkily when she gave an audible gasp of fury. 'I hope you sleep well, Freya, and don't have *too* restless a night.'

It was his superior smile that did it. Freya's anger burst the tight bands of her self-control and with a choked cry she snatched up a small glass ornament from the bureau and flung it at him. He fielded it expertly—of course, she thought bleakly as she fled along the hall to her room. Was there nothing that Zac didn't excel in? Or had he had plenty of practice in avoiding missiles that irate ex-lovers hurled at his head? It was not a comforting thought and burning up with mortification, she flung herself into bed, drew the covers over her head and wished she could dismiss the sound of his cruel laughter from her ears.

CHAPTER FOUR

FREYA was running down the hall of the penthouse with Aimee in her arms, searching for Zac. She could hear his voice ahead of her but the passageway seemed to go on for ever and he remained a distant figure who taunted her desperate attempts to catch up with him. Tears filled her eyes as she struggled on. Aimee was heavy and her wrist was agony, but it was nothing compared to the pain in her heart as she faced the knowledge that she would never reach Zac and she would always be alone…

'Freya—wake up.'

A familiar, terse voice sounded loud in her ear and when she opened her eyes she discovered that she was not in the hall, but her bedroom, and Zac was standing close to her bed regarding her with undisguised impatience.

'You were dreaming,' he told her when she stared up at him warily, her eyes huge and shadowed, unwittingly revealing a degree of vulnerability that caused Zac's frown to deepen. 'I suppose you're bound to suffer flashbacks from the accident.' He glanced at his watch and his mouth tightened. He had waited for Freya to wake up and was already behind schedule, but she looked achingly fragile this morning and he was irritated by his concern. 'Do you want to talk about it?' he queried, stifling his impatience when she simply stared at him in bemusement.

The strap of her nightdress had slipped off her shoulder and he recalled with stark clarity the way he had pushed it even lower last night, to leave her pale breast exposed. The sight of her dusky pink nipple had filled him with an uncontrollable longing to bend his head and take the hard peak in his mouth, suckle her until she whimpered with pleasure, and it had taken every vestige of his willpower to stop himself from pushing her back onto the sofa and covering her body with his own. The memory was enough to make him harden until he was sure she must see the embarrassing proof of his arousal, and, inhaling sharply, he took a jerky step back from the bed.

'Talk about what?' Freya asked him in genuine confusion. Her brain seemed to be made of cotton wool this morning and her thought process wasn't aided by the sight of Zac in a superbly tailored grey suit that emphasised the width of his broad shoulders. He looked urbane and sophisticated, every inch the billionaire businessman, and she was horribly aware of her dishevelled appearance. She adjusted the strap of her nightdress, her cheeks flaming when she caught the amused gleam in his eyes. She'd hoped that last night had all been part of her nightmare, but the tenderness of her swollen lips was proof that he had kissed her and she had responded with an enthusiasm that now made her shudder.

'The accident,' he snapped, forcing her to concentrate on him. 'You were crying in your sleep and it was obviously a terrifying experience. I've heard that it helps to talk,' he added stiffly, shrugging his shoulders in a gesture that indicated he had never been afraid in his life, let alone felt the need to confide his private emotions. Zac didn't suffer from the same human frailties as normal people, Freya thought bleakly. He spent most of his waking hours at work and regarded sex as a recreational activity that occupied his nights until he could return to his office the following day.

'I'm fine, thanks,' she murmured as she dragged her gaze from him and stared down at the bedcovers. She wondered what he would say if she revealed that she had been dreaming about him, not the accident, and that he had been the cause of her tears. He would be out of her room like a rabbit out of a trap, she thought grimly. Two years ago he had made it plain that he only wanted a physical relationship with her and, if she was ever insane enough to respond to the unspoken invitation in his eyes, she would have to remember that the rules hadn't changed.

But she would not respond to him ever again, she told herself firmly, tensing when he moved closer to the bed. His eyes glittered with the flames of desire and for one terrifying moment she thought he was going to reach out and touch her, but instead he dropped a piece of paper into her lap.

'The nurse is here to perform the mouth swabs,

but I require your signature before she can take a sample from Aimee,' he said bluntly. He moved away from the bed and stood with his back to her, staring out of the window while she quickly scanned the document. It seemed straightforward, but her heart was pounding as she added her signature. Now there was no going back. In ten days' time Zac would learn the truth, but how would he react when he was forced to accept that Aimee was his child?

She glanced at Zac's stern profile and bit her lip as she felt herself softening a little. He was a proud man and he was going to hate learning that he had been wrong about her.

He must have felt her silent scrutiny and swung round to face her, his eyes narrowing. 'Having second thoughts, Freya? I thought you might when you were faced with the reality of the paternity test,' he said coolly. 'But I want this test and if you refuse to give your permission, I'll go through the courts to get it. At the moment you're a loose cannon from my past, but once I have incontrovertible proof that you are a liar I'll take out a legal injunction if necessary to prevent you from ever approaching me or repeating your fantastic claims.'

Freya waved her signature at him furiously as the soft feeling vanished and was instantly replaced by a strong desire to commit murder—his. 'Far from having second thoughts, I was wishing I'd demanded a test as soon as Aimee was born,' she retorted. 'You've vilified and insulted me once too often, Zac, and the only thing that prevents me from slapping that smug expression from your face is the knowledge that the day will soon come when you'll fall from your lofty pedestal and have to acknowledge that you're a mere mortal like the rest of us—not the superior being you think you are.'

The glinting fury in his eyes warned her that she had pushed him too far, and she shrank back against the pillows when he snatched the consent form from her fingers and leaned over her, his hands on either side of her head. 'It appears that my meek little English mouse has developed a sharp tongue. Be careful it doesn't get you into trouble, *chérie*,' he warned dangerously as he lowered his head and captured her mouth in a stinging kiss that forced her head back. He took without mercy, dominating her with insulting ease and demanding that she part her lips for him so that he could slide his tongue deep into her mouth to continue his sensual punishment.

Freya's muscles locked and her mind screamed at her to reject him, but her body had a will of its own and she could feel its traitorous response as molten heat surged through her veins. Torn between hunger and humiliation, she groaned and he captured her despairing cry, grinding his lips on hers to prevent its escape. When he finally lifted his head she was beyond words and closed her eyes against the contempt she was sure she would see in his. She heard him swear savagely beneath his breath and tensed, waiting for the taunts that would surely follow, but there was nothing and at the slam of the bedroom door she lifted her lashes to find that he had gone.

Zac's visit had left Freya physically and emotionally drained and she lay back on the pillows, telling herself that she would get up in five minutes and go and check on Aimee. When she next woke up, sunshine was streaming into her room and she stared at the clock, horrified to see that it was mid-morning. How could she have slept for so long and not paid a single thought to her daughter? she berated herself angrily, but as she was about to get up she heard the sound of Aimee's high-pitched laughter and a moment later the nanny Zac had employed put her head round the door.

'Oh, you're awake. I've someone here who wants to see you,' Jean Lewis announced cheerfully as she opened the door wider and Aimee trotted into the room.

'Mrs Lewis, I'm so sorry, I never meant to sleep for so long,' Freya said quickly. She couldn't imagine what the nanny must think of her, but the older woman smiled reassuringly.

'It's Jean,' she said firmly, 'and of course you must sleep. Mr Deverell explained about your accident—it must have been a dreadful experience and, apart from your injuries, you're probably still in shock. Aimee's such a happy little girl and luckily she took to me straight away. I promise you, I'll take care of her as if she were my own,' she assured Freya with a friendly smile. 'If I were you, I'd spend the rest of the day in bed and I'll arrange for your meals to be brought to you.'

Freya didn't have the strength to argue. It felt strange to be mothered after the years of indifference from her grandmother, she mused after she had played with Aimee for a while before Jean Lewis had taken the little girl off to explore the roof-garden. She had warmed to Jean's kindness instantly and for the first time since Aimee's birth she felt she could relax and trust that her baby would be well cared for.

Over the next two days she began to appreciate Jean's advice. The accident had taken its toll and she was shocked at how tired and emotional she felt. The sound of laughter from the nursery indicated that Aimee was perfectly happy with the nanny, and it made a welcome change to have a temporary reprieve from her responsibilities.

To her relief she saw little of Zac. He had left for his office before she woke in the mornings and did not return until late in the evening. Some things hadn't changed, she mused wryly as she recalled the long, lonely days she had spent when she had lived with him, waiting for him to return from his office or one of his frequent business trips.

A few times he had taken her abroad with him. Deverell's owned stores in several European cities as well as New York, Rio de Janeiro and Dubai, but although the scenery was different her life had followed a similar pattern that had revolved around Zac and his hectic schedule.

She had been nothing more than a sex slave, she thought dismally, but innate honesty forced her to admit that she had taken on the role willingly. Zac had been like an addiction and at the time she had believed that she loved him. But had she confused love with lust? He had let her down so badly she could not possibly still be in love with him now, she reassured herself. The feelings he stirred in her were purely sexual. Although she hated herself, she wanted him with the same urgency that had consumed her when she had been his mistress. But she no longer believed in fairy tales, she would not mistake her physical awareness of him for a deeper emotion, and she certainly would not give in to this feverish need to allow him to make love to her.

Buoyed up by her newfound confidence that she could deal with Zac Deverell and his magnetic charm, Freya wandered through the lounge and out onto the wide balcony. Monaco was truly a billionaire's paradise, she mused as she stared down at the rows of luxury yachts and motor cruisers moored in the harbour. Zac enjoyed a glamorous lifestyle exclusive to the super-rich, but she had never felt comfortable with his wealth or fitted in with his friends.

In her heart she had always known that he was not the kind of man who would settle for a life of domestic bliss. Zac was an adventurer who lived life close to the edge with his love of extreme sports like sky-diving or power-boat racing. He got a buzz from pushing himself to the limits and playing happy families wasn't part of his game plan, as his rejection of her and their baby had demonstrated. In a few days he would learn that Aimee was his daughter, but she doubted he would sacrifice any part of his life for a child he didn't want.

With a heavy sigh she lifted her face to the sky and closed her eyes as the late-afternoon sunshine warmed her skin. After weeks of rain back in England, it felt wonderful, but her relaxed mood was shattered by a familiar voice from behind her.

'There you are. I've been looking everywhere for you,' Zac said, unable to disguise his impatience that she hadn't been instantly at his beck and call. 'I see you're keeping busy.'

Freya's eyes flew open and she glared at him indignantly. 'Aimee's having a nap and I had nothing to do for five minutes. You insisted that I should stay here,' she continued crossly when he said nothing. 'It's not my fault that there's nothing for me to do.' Her words were an eerie echo of the rows they used to have in the past, brought on by her loneliness and boredom and his refusal to cut down on his work schedule to spend time with her. Back then their arguments had ended with him sweeping her off to the bedroom to make love to her—and her capitulating at the first touch of his hands on her body, Freya thought grimly. But then she had given in too easily and now things were very different.

'Laurent informs me that you seem better

today,' Zac murmured as his eyes skimmed over her in blatant appreciation of her tight-fitting jeans and tee shirt. 'You certainly look good, *chérie*, although I can see that your injured wrist still prevents you from putting on your under-wear,' he added silkily.

Blushing furiously, Freya followed his gaze to the firm line of her breasts revealed beneath her thin cotton shirt and felt a tingling sensation as her nipples peaked provocatively beneath his stare. Electricity zinged between them and, despite the warmth of the sun, she shivered as each of her nerve endings flared into urgent life. With an angry murmur she swung away from him and stared out at the endless expanse of cobalt-blue sea.

'I am feeling better, and my wrist is already less painful—so much so that there's really no reason for me to stay here any longer. I've decided to take Aimee back to England while we wait for the test results,' she said.

'I'm afraid I can't allow that,' Zac said pleas-antly, but she caught the underlying note of steel in his voice and her temper flared.

'*Can't allow it?* Who do you think you are, Zac? I'm not your prisoner.'

'Certainly not.' He sounded insulted at the idea. 'You are my guest, although I admit that I took the liberty of locking your and Aimee's passports in my desk—in case you should lose them,' he added when she looked as though she were going to explode.

The breeze lifted her hair and blew the soft strands across his face, leaving behind the faint scent of lemons. Desire coiled low in his gut, but he resisted the urge to slide his fingers into her hair and carefully moved away from her. 'It suits me to keep you here until I have the results of the test,' he continued harshly, 'and then I shall personally escort you out of Monaco and out of my life, *chérie*. Until then I have a job for you, which should keep you occupied for a few hours at least.'

'You know what you can do with your damn job,' Freya choked, desperate to hide her devastation that he still had the ability to hurt her. Angry tears stung her eyes and she dashed them away with the back of her hand before swinging round to face him. 'You may have forced me to stay here, but you can't make me spend my time with you, let alone work for you.'

His mocking smile sent a frisson of alarm down her spine and she stepped back until she was jammed up against the balcony railings when he walked purposefully towards her. 'You should know by now that I can do whatever I like,' he said with breathtaking arrogance. 'And I'm not setting you to work down a salt mine. I'm having dinner tonight with an American businessman, Chester Warren, and his wife, followed by an evening at the Opera House to watch a performance by the Monte Carlo Ballet Company. My PA was supposed to be accompanying me but she's unwell. Francine is pregnant,' he told her with a grimace, 'and it seems that she suffers from morning sickness in the evenings.'

'Poor thing.' Freya nodded, forgetting her anger for a moment as she sympathised with Zac's PA. 'I was sick morning, noon and night for weeks when I was pregnant with Aimee.' She tailed to a halt beneath Zac's hard stare and a surge of bitterness flooded through her. Those first weeks after she had returned to England, pregnant, penniless and alone, had been the worst of her life as she had struggled with constant nausea and faced up to her future as a single mother. She had missed Zac desperately and begun every day hoping that he would realise he had made a mistake, and every night crying herself to sleep because he hadn't come for her. How dared he look at her with that faintly bored expression that told her he was completely disinterested in reminiscences about her pregnancy, when she had been carrying *his* child! 'I still don't understand what your PA's problems have to do with me,' she muttered stiffly.

'I need someone to take Francine's place tonight—you,' he confirmed, when she glared at him suspiciously. 'It will actually work out very well. Chester's wife Carolyn is English and I'm sure you'll be able to keep her entertained while Chester and I discuss business.'

'But…what do you expect me to talk to her about?' Freya asked, unable to hide the faint panic in her voice. She had never been good at small talk and trying to make conversation with people she'd never met before had been one of the things she'd hated when she had lived with Zac.

He shrugged his shoulders impatiently. 'I don't know. I'm sure you can swap stories about shopping in Bond Street or something.'

'Oh, yes—because I do that all the time.' She shook her head in exasperation. 'Zac, I honestly think that you and I come from different planets. I struggle to pay my bills and buy basic necessities while you live here in your gilded tower and have *no* idea of the real world.'

He didn't appear to be listening and had already swung away from her. Bristling with anger, she followed him into the lounge and stopped just inside the doorway, blinking as she stepped out of the bright sunlight on the balcony. 'I'm not coming with you. Find someone else to entertain your businessman and his wife.' She folded her arms across her chest and stared at him belligerently, frowning when he handed her a large flat box with the name of a well-known couture house on the front. 'What is this?'

'Something for you to wear tonight,' he replied blandly, seemingly unconcerned by her simmering temper or her refusal to accompany him to dinner.

Freya stared down at the box, her heart suddenly beating at twice its normal rate. 'You bought me a dress?' she said slowly, hating herself for the little thrill of pleasure she gained from the idea that he had taken time out of his busy schedule to go shopping for her.

'Actually, no, I gave Francine a rough idea of your size and she picked out a suitable outfit,' Zac instantly burst her bubble and she fell back to earth with a bump.

'Well, she wasted her time, because I'm not wearing it and I'm not going. What made you think I would agree?' she demanded furiously, her eyes widening at the sensual gleam in his.

'I was confident of playing on your sympathy for my secretary,' he said coolly, 'but, failing that, I can think of several other methods of persuasion that we'd both enjoy—although they may well result in us being late for dinner.' His slow smile triggered alarm bells and she bit back her retort as her mind fantasised about how he would bend her to his will. With ease, that was for sure, she acknowledged on a wave of self-disgust. Just the thought of his hands and mouth caressing her was enough to send liquid heat pooling between her thighs. If he touched her, kissed her again, she seriously doubted her ability to resist him—and he knew it.

She swallowed and tore her eyes from his mocking smile, tears of shame prickling behind her eyelids. If she wanted to retain any vestige of her self-respect, she would have to agree to go to dinner with him because she could not risk him *persuading* her.

'It was kind of your PA to go to so much trouble,' she said tightly, carefully not looking at him. 'And because I know how unwell she must be feeling at the moment, I'll agree to take her place tonight.' Clutching the box he had given her, she headed for the door, her back ramrod straight as his softly spoken comment followed her.

'I hadn't expected you to give in so easily, *chérie*. What a pity,' he drawled with genuine regret in his voice. 'I was looking forward to…coaxing you round to my way of thinking.'

* * *

Hours later Freya studied her reflection in the mirror. The dress Zac's secretary had chosen for her was a deceptively simple floor-length black sheath with a lace overlay, narrow shoulder straps and a neckline that plunged lower than Freya was happy with. When she had first realised how much of her cleavage was exposed she'd seriously considered changing into something else, but challenging Zac was not a good idea and she was afraid that if he tried to *coax* her, he would almost certainly win. Instead she had piled her hair on top of her head, and slipped on a pair of high-heeled sandals. Now, deciding she was ready, she swept out to meet Zac, her pulse rate quickening at the flare of undisguised desire in his eyes when he caught sight of her.

It gave her a fierce thrill of feminine triumph to realise that she was not the only one to be suffering from sexual frustration. Zac wanted her and was fighting the same battle to control his hunger. The knowledge empowered her and, instead of slinking shyly into the lounge, she sauntered confidently across the room, aware of his eyes lingering on the creamy swell of her breasts.

He looked breathtaking in his black tuxedo and white shirt that contrasted with his olive-gold skin, but for the first time she felt almost his equal and she met his gaze steadily as faint colour briefly highlighted his sharp cheekbones. The atmosphere in the room throbbed with tension and for one wild, crazy moment she wondered how he would react if she walked over to him and kissed his mouth with all the pent-up longing she was struggling to control.

Of course she did no such thing. She wasn't completely stupid and, besides, one kiss would not have been enough for either of them. What she really wanted was to feel the hard length of him deep inside her as he drove her to the pinnacle of sexual ecstasy—and that was never going to happen again, she reminded herself firmly.

She was shaken out of her erotic fantasies by his terse voice informing her that they had to leave, but she felt his brooding stare on her as they rode the lift down to the car park. The short journey to the hotel where they were meeting his American client was completed in silence, but once there Zac immediately exerted his usual charismatic charm as he ushered her into the bar and introduced her to Chester Warren and his wife.

From then on Freya concentrated on chatting to Carolyn Warren and struck up an instant rapport with the older woman when she discovered that she originated from a small Hampshire village, a few miles inland from Freya's home town. After cocktails at the hotel, they moved on to the wonderfully ornate Salle Garnier Opera House where the performance by the Monte Carlo Ballet Company was truly magical, and afterwards they returned to the hotel for a late dinner.

'So, Freya, do you like living here in Monaco?' Chester Warren queried when they had finished eating. 'Carolyn tells me you're from the same part of England where she was born—quaint little place, although I can never remember its name,' he added cheerfully.

Freya glanced across the dance floor to where Carolyn Warren was dancing with Zac. 'I love Monaco,' she replied, 'but I don't live here. I'm just a...friend of Zac's and I'm staying here with my daughter for a few days. I'll be going home soon,' she added, wondering why the thought caused a sick feeling in the pit of her stomach. She would be glad to get back to reality, she told herself firmly. She didn't belong here in this billionaire's playground and she had no place in Zac's life.

The bleakness in her voice caused Chester to stare at her with undisguised curiosity. 'Friends, eh,' he drawled. 'Well, Zac's a fine man—as charming as his father was and just as ruthless in the boardroom,' he said on a note of admiration. 'I remember when Charles died a couple of years back, there were some on the Deverell board who believed Zac wasn't up to the job of Chief Executive. He was seen as a playboy—you know, fast cars, plenty of women.' Chester chuckled. 'But to give him his dues, he worked like a dog to prove he was a worthy successor to his father even though he was pretty cut up at Charles' death. Now, of course, Deverell's profits are soaring and Zac has the full support of his board, but I hear he still works all the hours God sends.' Chester winked at her conspiratorially.

'Maybe he needs to get himself a wife, although he's shown no signs yet of wanting to settle down. I guess it would take a pretty special lady to tame him.'

'She would have to have the patience of a saint for a start,' Freya agreed tightly, despising herself for the way her heart lurched at the idea of Zac getting married.

'Why, *chérie*, you make me sound as though I'm an ogre,' an amused voice sounded in her ear and she swung her head round sharply, her eyes clashing with Zac's glinting gaze. 'I'm not that unbearable, am I?'

Cheeks flaming, Freya gave him a look that warned him he did not want to know her opinion of him, but to her annoyance he gave her one of his devastating smiles and tugged her to her feet before she could think of an excuse not to dance with him.

'I obviously need to demonstrate my charming side,' he murmured smoothly as he swept her across the dance floor.

'Forget it,' Freya snapped. 'I know exactly what you are, Zac, and your famous charm does nothing for me.' She tried to ease away from him but his arms tightened around her waist and she gave a shocked gasp when she felt the rigid proof of his arousal straining against her pelvis.

'You disappoint me, *ma petite*, especially as you can be in no doubt of what you're doing to me right now,' he said mockingly. He placed his hand in the small of her back and exerted enough pressure so that she was forced up against him.

'You are disgusting,' Freya hissed as she tried to ignore the warmth that was flooding through her. The music slowed and Zac steered her around the dance floor, each subtle movement of his hips bringing his aroused body into closer contact with hers. In desperation Freya closed her eyes against the scorching heat of his gaze, but the sensations he was arousing in her only intensified and she shuddered when his hand inched lower down her back and made small, circular movements across the top of her buttocks. She stumbled and clung to him as the music faded to the periphery of her mind. Nothing existed but Zac, and the subtle, sensuous rub of his hand evoked a delicious, quivering excitement between her thighs.

Without the barrier of their clothes he would be free to take her properly and thrust deep into her, she thought dreamily, the image of him doing just that suddenly so stark in her head that her muscles clamped and to her utter shock she felt tiny spasms of pleasure radiate from her central core. She felt Zac tense, but she couldn't prevent her climax and as she shook uncontrollably he dipped his head and captured her startled cry with his mouth.

It was over almost instantly and as she came down reality intruded, bringing with it the music and hubbub of voices from the dance floor. *Oh, God, what had she done?* Had anyone seen? And was it even possible to reach a sexual climax when he hadn't even touched her intimately? Dying with shame, she could not bear to look at him, but her eyes seemed drawn to him by a magnetic force. His face was a rigid mask, his skin stretched taut over the knife-edge of his cheekbones while his eyes gleamed with sensual promise beneath his heavy lids.

She stared up at him in desperation, silently daring him to comment as his lip curled into a slow, mocking smile.

'You *are* hungry, *chérie*,' he drawled softly. 'If I'd known I would have followed my instincts when I first saw you in that dress tonight and cancelled dinner.'

Freya swallowed her retort as he led her back to their table, aware that she was not in a position to say anything when her body had behaved so abominably. To her utter relief no one else in the room seemed to have noticed her making a spectacle of herself, but Zac would never let her forget her moment of weakness, she thought on a wave of panic. He knew now she was his for the taking whenever he chose. But somehow she would have to resist him before he damaged her self-esteem permanently.

CHAPTER FIVE

IT WAS almost midnight when they bid Chester and Carolyn Warren goodnight and drove back to the penthouse. Freya wished she were tired but to her dismay she felt wide awake and filled with a wild, reckless energy. Those few moments of madness on the dance floor with Zac had inflamed her senses and left her body aching for his full possession—but it was going to be disappointed.

She intended to go straight to her room the moment they entered the apartment, but Zac's butler, Laurent, greeted them with a tray of coffee and *petits fours* that he had prepared specially for their return. 'I'd really like to go to bed,' she muttered to Zac as he ushered her into the lounge in the wake of the butler.

'And upset Laurent?' His eyebrows raised a notch. 'You're a brave woman.'

Stifling a groan, she dredged up a smile and accepted a cup of frothy cappuccino from the butler. The last thing she needed right now was the additional stimulation of caffeine, she thought gloomily as she watched Zac drain his cup in two gulps before he crossed to the bar and poured himself a cognac.

'Would you like a nightcap with your coffee?'

'No, thank you,' she replied hastily. What she needed was something to knock her senseless for the next twelve hours and prevent her disturbing fantasies about Zac, but, although getting blind drunk was tempting, she decided that her loss of control tonight had been embarrassing enough to last her a lifetime.

She stirred her coffee and glanced up at Zac, who was standing at the window staring out into the darkness. 'When did your father die?' she asked him quietly, recalling her conversation with Chester Warren. 'Chester said it was two years ago, which was when we met, but you never said anything and I had no idea you were grieving.'

Zac shrugged dismissively. 'My father died nine months before I met you and my grief was a private matter which was nothing to do with you or our relationship.'

He sounded so cold, so clinical, that Freya shivered. Zac kept his life compartmentalised into separate boxes and had clearly never considered allowing her into the box marked personal. 'But if you'd told me I might have been able to…I don't know—' she broke off helplessly '—help in some way.'

'How?' he demanded tersely. 'You couldn't have brought him back and I did not need help. I dealt with my grief.' He had neither looked for, nor wanted, sympathy, he brooded grimly, and he had been determined to deal with the loss of his father in his own way, which for the most part had been to block it out of his mind and get on with his life.

After his twin sisters had died a few months after birth, his mother had sunk into a deep depression that had lasted for most of his adolescence. He had been shocked by the power of love and had viewed it as a destructive emotion that had wreaked havoc on his parents' lives, and he had decided that he would never be held hostage to his emotions.

When his father died, his mother had been distraught and once again he had felt helpless in the face of her overwhelming grief. But Freya's soft smile and unashamedly eager sensuality had been a welcome relief from the surfeit of Yvette Deverell's emotions. He hadn't wanted to talk about grief or loss; he had wanted to forget everything and enjoy her glorious body—until he'd discovered that she hadn't been giving herself exclusively to him.

Zac's shuttered expression warned Freya that he did not welcome her intrusion into an area of his life that he had never spoken of before, but she pushed on doggedly, determined to learn more about this man who was to all intents and purposes still a stranger to her. 'Chester told me that you felt you had to work particularly hard to prove to the Deverell board that you would be a worthy successor to your father. If you had explained why you practically lived at your office, I would have understood,' she insisted.

'But instead you grew bored of waiting for me and looked elsewhere for sex.' Zac gave a harsh laugh. '*Mon Dieu*, I satisfied you every night, but it wasn't enough, was it, *chérie*? You were insatiable, you wanted me on hand morning, noon and night, and when I didn't give you enough attention you acted like a spoilt brat.'

'It wasn't like that,' Freya defended herself. 'I wanted us to have a normal life like other couples, to spend weekends together and the occasional evenings rather than you coming home at midnight and taking me to bed like I was a…a whore you paid to pleasure you.' She set down her coffee-cup with a clatter, her whole body tensing in rejection when Zac strode across the room and stood, towering over her.

'But that's exactly what you were,' he said savagely. 'I kept you as my mistress and paid for every conceivable luxury you could want, in return for your…services.' The withering contempt in his eyes as he stared down at her made her feel sick and she shook her head wildly.

'I never asked you to buy me clothes and jewellery. I never asked you for anything, apart from your time. I wanted you, Zac, not the things you could give me,' she whispered, but he snorted impatiently and dropped down onto the sofa next to her, trapping her against the cushions.

'I know exactly what you wanted, and when you decided that you weren't getting enough from me, you slept with your foppish artist.'

'I did not sleep with Simon.' Hurt and frustration exploded inside her and she lashed out at him, only to have him capture her hands and drag her across his lap.

'The bodyguard saw you,' he said with a steely calm that alarmed her more than if he had shouted at her. His eyes were hard and utterly implacable and she gasped in shock when he caught hold of the straps of her dress and dragged them down her arms with such force that the material ripped. The bodice of her dress instantly slipped down, leaving her breasts exposed, and when she fought manically to free herself from his hold he pushed her so that she was lying flat on her back.

'Zac, don't,' she pleaded fearfully, terrified not of him but of herself and the certainty that she would not be able to resist him. His barely leashed savagery only added to her feverish excitement and, although she hated herself, she could feel her body's treacherous response when he skimmed his hands over her ribcage and cupped her breasts in his palms.

'Don't deny that you want me, Freya,' he warned softly. 'Not after what happened on the dance floor tonight. You don't know how close I was to spreading you across the nearest table and taking you in front of a room full of onlookers,' he growled, his voice thick and his accent heavily pronounced as he relived those few seconds when she had trembled in his arms. The shocked confusion in her green eyes had driven him to the edge and since then his arousal had been a throbbing force that he was impatient to assuage.

'That shouldn't have happened,' she muttered, her face flaming. 'It was just a horribly embarrassing physical reaction. I haven't dated anyone since we split up. Even if I'd wanted to, I couldn't when I had Aimee to care for. But I have the same urges as anyone else.' Although it seemed that only Zac could satisfy those urges, she conceded bleakly. If he could bring her to a climax simply by dancing with her, what chance did she stand if he decided to make love to her properly? she wondered despairingly. But it no longer seemed to matter; his hands were gently moulding her breasts and now his thumb pads were stroking across the tight peaks of her nipples, backwards and forwards until the pleasure was almost unbearable and she felt a sharp tug of desire.

This was dangerous territory and she should beat a retreat, her brain warned, but a curious weakness seemed to have invaded her limbs and she could do nothing but watch as he lowered his head and flicked his tongue across one sensitive crest. With a low cry she put out her hands to push him away, but her wayward fingers strayed to his shirt buttons and worked them free before she pushed the material aside and revelled in the feel of his warm golden skin beneath her fingertips.

It had been so long since she had touched him. She loved the solid strength of his chest and powerful shoulders—loved him, whispered a tiny voice in her head. She was his, totally, and she murmured her approval when he transferred his mouth to her other breast and drew her nipple fully into his mouth. The exquisite sensation built on the need that had begun on the dance floor and was now a greedy, clamouring ache to feel him inside her.

Zac stared down at her flushed face and muttered something beneath his breath before he claimed her mouth in a kiss of pure possession, drawing a response from her that she could no longer deny. A tremor ran through his big body and he tore his mouth from hers to drag her dress over her hips. He loved watching her unguarded response to him and held her gaze as he drew her knickers down and pushed her thighs apart with deliberate intent.

Her eyes darkened to the colour of a stormy sea and she made a little half murmur of protest when he ran his hand through the soft blonde curls and then parted her and slid his fingers deep into her.

Freya held her breath, torn between the need for him to continue his wickedly intimate caresses and the dictates of her pride, which were telling her that she must stop this madness now, before it was too late. But Zac was a master of seduction and his skilful fingers continued to move inside her, while his thumb pad stroked with delicate precision over her ultra sensitive clitoris, building her excitement so that she twisted restlessly and tried to control the delicious spasms that were threatening to overwhelm her.

'Zac…' His eyes were focused on her face and there was something shockingly erotic about the way he was watching her while he pleasured her. She was going to die of shame in the cold light of day, but his fingers were moving faster in a sensual dance and with a groan she tipped her head back as wave after wave of incredible sensation tore through her. Only then did he lower his head once more to capture her mouth in a slow, drugging kiss, his tongue dipping between her lips as he mimicked the actions his fingers had performed seconds before.

'Tell me, *chérie*, am I the only man who can turn you on like that, or will anyone do when you're desperate—Brooks, for example?' Zac's coldly mocking voice shattered the sexual haze and Freya tensed as pain ripped her apart. His opinion of her hadn't changed; he still regarded her as unfaithful and his readiness to believe the worst of her was unbearable. Her desire drained away, leaving her so cold that her teeth chattered, and when his hand moved to the zip of his trousers she felt sick with misery.

'Don't,' she pleaded through numb lips, her eyes huge and overbright in her white face. 'I don't think I could bear it. You've made your point, Zac, and we both know that I'm pathetically incapable of resisting you. But if you make love to me tonight I think I might hate you almost as much as I hate myself.'

For a few mindless seconds, Zac was tempted to ignore her. He had never wanted a woman the way he wanted her, never been held at the mercy of such a gnawing hunger that caused a cramping pain in his gut. He was in agony, damn it, and he knew he could make it good for her too. But the glimmer of her tears was getting to him, even though he despised women who were able to turn on the waterworks whenever it suited them. Freya was not one of those women, he conceded grimly, and the stark vulnerability in her eyes unearthed a flare of compassion in him that he'd never known he possessed.

With a furious oath he jerked away from her, his nostrils flaring with the effort of controlling his urge to take her. 'Cover yourself and get out,' he growled, flinging her dress at her before he strode over to the bar. He'd known from the moment he stood by her hospital bed that she would be trouble and he couldn't fathom what madness had made him bring her back here. The day couldn't come too soon when he would be able to dismiss her from his life for ever, he thought savagely as he slugged back his drink and poured himself another. But when he swung round to tell her, she had gone.

Freya leaned over the cot and brushed her lips over Aimee's velvety soft cheek. The toddler's lashes were already drifting down and within seconds she was asleep, worn out from an energetic afternoon playing with Jean Lewis in the roof-garden.

Jean had become a firm friend of both mother and daughter and they would miss her warmth and kindness when they returned to England, Freya mused sadly. And that day was drawing ever closer. It was over a week since Zac had brought them to Monaco and any day now he would receive the results of the paternity test. She predicted that his reaction would not be good and had already decided that she would take Aimee home immediately.

'I thought she'd drop off quickly,' Jean said cheerfully when Freya tiptoed from the nursery. 'She loves playing outside, although she was very cross when I insisted that she wear her sunhat.'

'You're so good with her,' Freya said with a smile. 'I thought she was going to have a tantrum about the hat, but you managed to distract her.'

Jean chuckled. 'I've had years of practice dealing with toddler tantrums, and really Aimee is so well behaved. She's an adorable child.' She paused and then added, 'What a beautiful dress. You look lovely Freya.'

'Thank you.' Freya glanced down at the elegant cocktail dress that had been one of her favourites when she had lived with Zac. The green silk crêpe de Chine clung to her slender curves and the colour looked good against the light tan she had acquired while playing in the sunshine with Aimee.

Zac was hosting a dinner party tonight and had curtly informed her that, as his PA was still feeling unwell, he required her to act as his hostess. She was looking forward to the evening with as much enthusiasm as a trip to an abattoir. Relations between them had improved marginally since their last explosive confrontation, but only because she avoided him whenever possible.

It wasn't difficult; he had always left for his office before she was up and he returned late—or not at all, she thought grimly. Common sense told her he was bound to have a mistress in Monaco. He possessed a high sex drive and, although he had respected her wishes and held back from making love to her after the evening they had spent with the Warrens, she had been in no doubt of his frustration.

But there were plenty of women who would willingly satisfy his needs and all week her imagination had kept her awake at night as she had pictured him with some nubile beauty. Jealousy was a corrosive emotion. She hated herself as she lay awake each night listening for his key in the lock and hated him more when dawn brought with it the bitter realisation that he had spent the night in another woman's bed.

The results of the DNA test couldn't come soon enough, she thought miserably. Living under the same roof as Zac was destroying her self-respect. She had no idea what he would do when he discovered that she hadn't been unfaithful to him, and she no longer cared, she realised. Possibly he would offer to pay maintenance for Aimee, but it was unlikely that he would want any kind of contact with his daughter and with luck she would never have to see him again.

She found him in the lounge, staring out at the spectacular view over the bay. In a formal dinner suit he looked more gorgeous than ever. The expertly tailored jacket moulded the formidable width of his shoulders and when he swung round she noted the way his brilliant white shirt accentuated his olive-gold skin.

'Freya.' he studied her in silence for a few moments, his brows drawn into a slashing frown. '*Mon Dieu!* You have a nerve wearing *that* dress.

Did you do so expressly to anger me? Because if so, you've succeeded.'

Startled by his barely leashed aggression, Freya shook her head. 'You told me to wear the clothes I'd left behind when you…' she bit down on her lip as bitter memories came hurtling back '…when you threw me out.'

'True, but I didn't expect you to parade around in the very dress you were wearing on the night you tried to seduce me into believing the child you were carrying was mine,' he hissed contemptuously.

Had she really worn this dress on the worst night of her life? Freya's brow knotted as she tried to remember, but all she could recall was Zac's savage condemnation of her. At the beginning of that fateful evening she *had* dressed to please him, but after it had all gone so spectacularly wrong she had fled to her dressing room and hastily changed into her jeans before he had ignominiously evicted her from the penthouse.

'I didn't try to seduce you,' she said, her temper flaring when she saw the acrid condemnation in his eyes.

'Non?' He gave a harsh laugh as he strolled towards her with a lithe grace that reminded her of a panther stalking its kill. 'I remember the way you flew into my arms the moment I stepped through the door. We were supposed to be going out to dinner but you clung to me. I couldn't resist you, *chérie*, and you knew it, but you overplayed your hand when you thought you could fool me into believing your lies.'

He was so close that she could *feel* the anger emanating from his body and when she tilted her head to look up at him, the stark emotion in his eyes made her tremble. Passion and fury— together they were a volatile mixture that filled her with trepidation and an undeniable excitement that had been building all week. She recognised his hunger; saw the way his eyes darkened with desire, and when his head descended she stood stock still, like a hare trapped in the headlights of a speeding car, waiting for the inevitable.

Voices from the hall shattered the haze of sexual tension and he jerked back from her, muttering a savage oath beneath his breath. 'My guests are here and it's too late for you to change now. But be aware, *chérie*, that every time I look at you tonight I'll be imagining you with Brooks.' His deliberate crudity made her wince, but when she attempted to move away from him he slid his arm around her waist and held her in a vice like grip. 'Why aren't you wearing the support bandage on your wrist?' he demanded roughly.

'I thought I'd manage without it for a couple of hours.' The butler, Laurent, was heading down the hall followed by Zac's guests and, despite feeling as though her heart had been put through a pulping machine, she forced a brittle smile. 'At least the necessity to go and put it on again will give me a reason to excuse myself from your vile company.'

From that moment on the evening became a hellish ordeal that Freya longed to end. Fortunately no one attending the dinner had known her during the few months she had lived with Zac and awkward explanations were avoided. His guests were frighteningly sophisticated but friendly—although in some cases, too friendly, she thought darkly when she caught sight of him deep in conversation with an attractive brunette. Mimi Joubert had arrived alone, but from the easy familiarity she shared with Zac it seemed likely that she would not be returning home tonight.

Freya swallowed the bile that burned her throat and forced herself to smile at the man at her side. Lucien Giraud had also arrived at the dinner party unaccompanied, but Freya was sure that had been through choice rather than because he could not find a date. He was good-looking and charming and had flirted with her outrageously throughout dinner. Fearful of appearing rude, she had called on all her acting skills to respond warmly to him, but her laughter had disguised the misery that swamped her every time she felt Zac's eyes on her. The blistering contempt in his gaze reminded her of his taunt that he was picturing her with Simon Brooks and she felt the crazy urge to jump onto the table and shout out her innocence. It would certainly be the talking point of the evening, she thought bitterly.

By midnight, she'd had enough. She was fast running out of patience with Lucien's none-too-

subtle attempts to place his hand on her thigh—
the man had an ego the size of Mount Everest—
and she glared at him when he leaned close and
whispered in her ear.

'So, Freya, what will it take to persuade you to
have dinner with me?' he murmured seductively,
clearly convinced that the route from the dining
room to his bedroom would be completed in
minimum time.

'More than you can imagine,' Freya replied
sharply, trying to edge along the sofa when she
felt his gaze settle on her cleavage. 'I'm afraid
you'll have to excuse me,' she said as she slapped
away his roaming hand and jumped to her feet.
'My arm is beginning to ache and I need to take
some painkillers. It was nice to meet you,' she
lied, stifling an impatient groan when Lucien
stood and captured her hand.

'It has been a pleasure for me also, Freya,' he
replied, lifting her hand to his mouth with a
theatrical flourish that caught the attention of
everyone in the room. 'I hope very much that we
will meet again.'

Not in this lifetime—if she could help it, Freya

vowed silently as she repeated her excuse for leaving the party to the other guests and hurried from the room, acutely conscious of Zac's gaze burning like a laser between her shoulder blades. As his hostess she supposed she should have remained on hand until his guests departed, but watching him smile and flirt with Miss Joubert was sheer agony and she couldn't stand another five minutes of it.

Despite Freya feeling bone-weary, sleep proved elusive and two hours later she gave up her restless tossing beneath the sheets and headed for the kitchen to make a milky drink. She had heard Zac's guests depart soon after she'd left the party, but the light streaming from beneath his bedroom door and the muted sound of a woman's voice caused her to pause in the hallway. Obviously not everyone had gone home. The image of Zac and the gorgeous Mimi Joubert filled her with sick misery and she stumbled on towards the kitchen feeling as though she had been kicked in the stomach.

Oh, God! How could it hurt so much? After all

this time and all the terrible accusations he had flung at her? She wanted to cry like a baby and tears blinded her as she poured milk into a saucepan and set it on the hob to heat. Of course he had a lover. There had probably been a steady stream of sophisticated beauties in his bed during the past two years—but the stark reality that he was at this moment making love to another woman was more than she could bear.

She mopped her wet face frantically with a paper towel. It was time she toughened up and stopped being so pathetic. She had coped with rejection all her life—she should be used to it by now, she thought bleakly, recalling the years of her childhood when she had tried so hard to win her grandmother's love. But Nana Joyce hadn't wanted her any more than her mother had done, and Zac had never made any pretence that he loved her. It was her own stupid fault that she had given him her heart and it should have come as no surprise that he had treated it with callous disregard.

Too late she heard the hiss of scalding hot milk as it frothed onto the hob. With a cry she grabbed the saucepan handle as a smell of burning filled the kitchen and, to her horror, the smoke alarm activated.

'What the hell are you playing at? I thought you were in bed.'

'I couldn't sleep.' Freya jerked her gaze from Zac's furious face and ran cold water over the ruined pan while he reached up and switched off the alarm. His hair was ruffled and his robe loosely fastened, as if he had leapt up from bed and dragged it around him. He looked indecently sexy and the knowledge that he was naked beneath the black silk caused her heart to thud unevenly.

'That's no reason to wake the rest of the household,' he said tersely, his eyes narrowing as he noted the streaks of tears on her face.

'I'm sorry—I didn't mean to disturb you,' she muttered miserably, unable to dismiss the picture of him tearing himself out of Mimi Joubert's arms. 'I think the pan's salvageable if I scrub it.'

'Leave it.' He snatched the pan that she had filled with soapsuds and, infuriated by his high-handedness, she grabbed it back again.

'Let me do it. Go back to bed. You don't want to keep Miss Joubert waiting,' she hissed beneath her breath, and then gasped when he forcibly removed the saucepan from her hand and spun her round to face him.

'What?' His tone was deceptively mild, but the glinting fury in his gaze warned that he had reached the limits of his patience.

'Miss Joubert—I know she's staying with you,' Freya murmured uneasily, trying to edge away from him and finding herself jammed up against the worktop. 'I don't care,' she told him sharply, terrified that he might think she was jealous. Her cheeks burned when he continued to stare at her speculatively, as if he could see inside her head. 'We're both free agents and you can sleep with who you like.'

'*Merci, chérie,*' he murmured sardonically, 'but I have no plans to leap into bed with a business acquaintance I met for the first time a few days ago.' He paused for a heartbeat and then said softly, 'It was clear from your behaviour with Lucien Giraud this evening that you do not feel bound by the same constraints of moral propriety.'

'Meaning what, precisely?'

'Meaning that you were all over him like a

rash,' he growled, his face twisting in distaste. 'You're not even fully recovered from your injuries, and yet you waste no time trying to seduce another wealthy lover. Perhaps you are already preparing for the outcome of the DNA test,' he sneered, 'and are intending to sell yourself to Giraud in return for financial security for you and your child.'

His cruel taunt pierced her heart and in an agony of hurt she brought her hand up to meet his cheek with a resounding crack. For a few seconds she stared at him in horror, and then closed her eyes as a wave of shame and nausea swept over her. She deplored physical violence, but how dared he insinuate that she was no better than a whore? The blazing fury in his eyes warned that she had pushed him too far and with a cry she shot down the hall, but had only gone a few paces before he caught hold of her and swung her into his arms.

'Take your hands off me!' She pummelled her fists against his chest and gasped when he marched determinedly towards his room. 'If you're planning a threesome, you can damn well think again.' Burning up with embarrassment, she screwed her eyes shut when he strode through the door and deposited her on the bed. Surely she had plumbed the depths of humiliation? she thought wildly, convinced that Zac and his beautiful bed-mate must be laughing at her.

But when she cautiously lifted her lashes there was only Zac staring down at her—no hint of amusement on his face, just stark, primitive hunger and an implacable determination in his eyes that sent alarm feathering down her spine.

CHAPTER SIX

'I AM a patient man,' Zac stated with a mind-boggling disregard for the truth, 'but I've had as much as I'm prepared to take from you.'

Frozen to the bed, Freya watched him activate the remote to turn off the television, before his hands moved to the belt of his robe. 'Obviously I was wrong about Miss Joubert. I'm sorry,' she muttered thickly. She watched him with wide, disbelieving eyes, her blood pounding in her veins when he loosened the belt and shrugged out of his robe to stand before her, gloriously and unashamedly naked.

'Zac!' She swallowed hard and tried to tear her gaze from the masculine perfection of his body. His skin gleamed like polished bronze in the lamplight and her eyes skittered down over the rippling muscles of his abdomen, following the path of dark hairs that arrowed down his taut stomach to his thighs. He was aroused—and it was the sight of his boldly erect manhood that finally penetrated the fog clouding her brain. 'What are you doing?'

'Taking what you were so blatantly offering to Lucien Giraud,' he replied coolly, foiling her attempt to scramble off the bed by coming down beside her and pinning her to the mattress with insulting ease.

'I was not.' Tears stung her eyes at the contempt in his, but her traitorous body recognised its soul mate and molten heat surged through her veins, leaving her weak with longing. One look was all it took to arouse her to fever pitch—what chance did she stand if he touched her, kissed her...? 'Zac, I don't want this.' She twisted her head frantically from side to side, her breath coming in shallow gasps.

'Liar.' His supreme self-confidence was mortifying, but when he captured her chin and slowly lowered his head, she shook with need and parted her lips to accept the savage mastery of his kiss.

The bold thrust of his tongue into her mouth should have appalled her, but she was drowning in sensation, her senses set aflame by his potent male heat. After the lonely years apart he was impossible to resist and with a groan she slid her arms around his neck, loving the feel of his silky hair against her fingers.

Sensing her capitulation, he eased the pressure of his mouth a little so that the kiss became a sensual, evocative tasting that brought fresh tears to her eyes. He was everything to her, the only man she had ever loved, but she meant nothing to him. It destroyed the last vestiges of her pride to accept that, even though he despised her, she wanted to make love with him one last time—a precious memory to cling to during all the bleak years ahead.

Zac trailed his lips down her throat, his fingers tugging the ribbons at the front of her negligee before he pushed the delicate peach-coloured satin aside to expose her breasts to his hungry gaze. His eyes darkened as he brushed his thumb across her nipple and watched her pupils dilate. 'I love the way you are so responsive, *chérie*,' he said roughly. 'There's no pretence with you, is there? You are the most sensual woman I have ever met and I have never been able to get you out of my blood.'

She tensed, sure that he was taunting her and expecting him to flay her with his sarcasm, but instead he lowered his head and the feel of his tongue drawing moist circles around her areola made her tremble with anticipation. He moved slowly, inexorably towards the centre until his mouth closed around the tight peak of her nipple and she gave a low cry as sensation pierced her. She arched up to him and clutched his shoulders while he teased her and tormented her, and just when she thought she could bear no more he transferred his mouth to her other breast and pleasured her until she was a limp mass of quivering need.

'You want me, Freya, and, God help me, I can't fight my hunger for you any more,' Zac growled as he tugged her negligee down over her hips and followed its path with his mouth on her skin—trailing kisses over the sensitive flesh of her stomach to the tiny triangle of peach satin that hid her femininity from his gaze.

It was purely physical, he reassured himself, his senses flaring when he caught the subtle, feminine scent of her arousal. The sexual attraction between them had always been explosive and, even though he knew she was a cold-blooded liar, he couldn't resist her. Her skin felt like silk beneath his fingertips and she was so soft and pliant that he had to restrain himself from plunging into her and taking her with primitive passion.

Drawing a sharp breath, he fought to leash his rampaging hormones as he slid his fingers beneath the lacy edge of her knickers. He pushed the material aside before he lowered his head and stroked his tongue lightly up and down the delicate folds of her femininity, coaxing and teasing until she whimpered and shifted her hips to allow him access to the moist heat within.

Freya knew she should stop him, but her limbs felt heavy and her entire body throbbed with desire. She couldn't do this again, couldn't give herself to a man whose opinion of her was rock-bottom. But Zac was the only man she had ever wanted and she couldn't deny him, not when it meant denying herself the exquisite pleasure of his possession.

His wickedly intrusive tongue seemed intent on destroying her self-control as he brought her to the brink and she gasped, part relief, part disappointment, when he suddenly lifted his head and stared down at her. 'You can't do this,' she whispered, shaken by the glittering contempt in his eyes when he removed her knickers with brisk efficiency. 'You think I'm a cheat and a liar,' she reminded him desperately, her eyes widening when he reached into the bedside drawer and took out a condom. He made no reply as he fitted it with practised ease and her heart thudded in her chest when he pushed her legs apart and moved over her. 'How can you make love to a woman you despise?' she cried jerkily, trembling with hurt and the frantic need to feel him inside her. She made one last despairing effort to halt him by beating her hands on his shoulders until he caught hold of her wrists and forced her arms above her head.

'Unfortunately you're not the only one to suffer from an embarrassing physical reaction,' he mockingly reminded her of the excuse she had made after she had climaxed in his arms on the dance floor. 'My brain tells me you're a tramp, but my body isn't so fastidious—it's just hungry,' he said grimly as he slid his hand under her bottom, lifted her and effected one deep, shockingly powerful thrust that made her gasp in awe at his potent strength.

It had been a long time since she had done this, but the ministrations of his hands and mouth had brought her to the peak of sexual arousal and she welcomed the full, rigid length of him as he slowly filled her. As her muscles stretched around him to form a tight, velvet sheath, Zac gave a low growl of satisfaction, eased back a fraction and then thrust again and again, setting a rhythm that she eagerly matched.

Each strong, deep stroke was sending Freya closer to the edge and she lost all sense of time and place as his male scent swamped her senses while the only sounds she could hear were her breathless cries for him to thrust faster and harder.

'I'll hurt you,' he muttered against her throat

when she wrapped her legs around his back and urged him on.

In the dim recess of her mind she recognised the truth of his words—not that she feared he would cause her physical pain, but emotionally he had the power to destroy her. But she blanked out the thought as her whole being focused on the exquisite sensations that were unfurling deep inside her. 'You won't,' she assured him huskily as she arched her hips in mute supplication for him to loosen his hold on his self-control and take her with the primitive force she knew he was capable of. 'I want you, Zac…I want…' The rest of her words were lost beneath the pressure of his mouth as he captured her lips in a fierce, drugging kiss that drove everything but her desperate need for fulfilment from her mind.

Zac's shoulders and brow were beaded with sweat and his face was a taut mask. He was a skilful lover who knew exactly how to give pleasure, but the time for playful seduction was long past and he was driven by a basic urge to satisfy his hunger. He slid his hands down Freya's slim body and gripped her buttocks as he drove into her, his jaw clenched as he felt her muscles contract around him.

He could feel his pleasure building to a crescendo, but just when he feared he could hold back no longer, she gave a sharp cry and her whole body convulsed beneath him in a shattering climax. The sensuous pleasure-pain of her nails raking down his back tipped him over the edge and he paused for an instant before giving one last forceful thrust that annihilated his control and sent shock waves through him as his body shuddered with the power of his release.

Freya clung to Zac's sweat-damp body and revelled in the weight of him as the lingering ripples of sensation drained from her. Recriminations were already mustering in her head, taunting her with her abject stupidity, but she was determined to ignore them for a few more blissful minutes. She could feel Zac's heartbeat thudding through her and she screwed her eyes shut and breathed in his musky, male scent. Making love with him topped the list of mistakes she had made—in her life that seemed littered with them—but she couldn't regret it.

Despite his mistrust and suspicion and his unshakeable opinion of her, she loved him, she acknowledged sadly, and it seemed likely that she always would.

Eventually he rolled off her to lay flat on his back, his silence growing more ominous to her ears by the second.

'I've decided that I want you back,' he said in a voice devoid of all emotion, 'to live here as my mistress the way we once were.' He turned his head on the pillows and stared at her coldly. 'You're like a drug in my veins and, although I despise myself, I seem to be addicted to you,' he grated harshly. 'I'm prepared to overlook your…indiscretion with Brooks, and if you stay I'll accept your child and provide for her as if she were my own. But if you ever look at another man the way you looked at Lucien Giraud tonight, so help me, *chérie*, I will not be responsible for my actions.'

For a few seconds Freya stared at him in stunned silence while her brain assimilated his words. Bitterness, humiliation and rage congealed her blood and she closed her eyes for a moment, shocked by the level of pain he could still inflict on her. How could she love him when he seemed determined to shred her heart into a thousand pieces? She obviously possessed a masochistic streak, she thought as agony swept through her.

'If—*overlooking my indiscretion with Brooks*—is your way of saying that you forgive me for having sex with Simon, you're wasting your breath,' she said tightly, her voice shaking with emotion. 'At a risk of repeating myself, I never slept with him or anyone else—ever.' She pushed against his chest with a force borne of desperation, terrified that she was actually going to be sick. 'How dare you! How *dare* you take that high and mighty tone with me? Your arrogance sickens me—*you* sicken me,' she flung at him.

All this time she'd struggled as a single mother, juggling work and childcare and using her few precious hours of free time while Aimee slept to study for her degree, in the hope that she could improve her financial situation. And all the while Zac had lived here in his luxury penthouse apartment, refusing to accept that he was the father of her child while he thought the worst of her. Not for much longer, she thought furiously. The results of the DNA test would force him to accept the truth and she hoped he suffered an overdose of remorse when he realised how cruelly he had misjudged her.

He was staring at her through narrowed eyes, his jaw tense, but she no longer felt overawed by him. Her pride had finally come to her rescue and, although it was way too late to salvage her self-respect, she had to try. With jerky movements she dragged her negligee over her head, ignoring the pain in her wrist. The pain in her heart was a thousand times worse and she scrambled to her feet, desperate to escape before she broke down in front of him. 'I don't need anything from you, Zac, certainly not your arrogant assertion that you'll overlook something I didn't even do,' she told him fiercely. 'But one day soon you'll come crawling to me on your hands and knees, and hear me now—I will *never* forgive you for your treatment of me.'

* * *

Freya woke with a start as sunlight filtered through the blinds and slanted across her face. Dazedly she stared at the clock on her beside table and gave a disbelieving frown—surely it couldn't really be ten a.m.? She sat up and groaned as she quickly fastened the front of her nightgown, her cheeks flaming when she recalled how Zac had stripped her last night before he had pushed her flat on her back and taken her with a savagery that had escalated her excitement to fever pitch.

What did that make her? she wondered dismally as she recalled her wanton response to him. And how could she have been so stupid and so utterly lacking in pride? He had looked down his arrogant nose at her while he'd stated that he was prepared to overlook her affair with Simon Brooks, but she was *innocent* and his lack of faith hurt as much now as it had two years ago. Every day that she spent with him he stripped away another layer of her protective shell, leaving her raw and vulnerable, and she knew she had to leave before the damage to her heart was irreparable.

A hesitant tap on the door heralded the arrival

of the maid. 'Ah, you are awake,' Elise said with a smile. 'Shall I bring you breakfast in bed?'

'No, thank you, Elise.' Freya jumped to her feet. 'Where is my daughter?'

'She is in the pool with Monsieur Deverell.'

Freya snatched up her robe and paused on the way to the *en suite* to stare blankly at the maid. 'Zac has taken Aimee swimming?' she queried, her voice sounding sharp as panic and confusion mingled. To her chagrin, Aimee had developed an instant fascination with Zac and, to give him credit, he treated the little girl with a gentle patience that he never revealed to anyone else—certainly not her, Freya thought bleakly.

Elise nodded. 'Madame Lewis is with them. Monsieur Deverell said that you'd had a disturbed night, and should be left alone to sleep,' she told Freya innocently. 'I'll tell him you are awake now. He wishes to see you in his study as soon as you are dressed.'

The temptation to pass on a message to Zac telling him to go to hell was so strong that Freya had to bite her lip. It wasn't fair to involve the penthouse staff in their private war, she reminded herself, and had to be content with cursing him beneath her breath as she stormed into the bathroom.

After the quickest shower on record, she dressed in a simple skirt and blouse suitable for travelling in, although her injured wrist still made it impossible for her to fasten her bra. She packed the few belongings she had brought from England and moved into the nursery where she swiftly stowed Aimee's clothes into a holdall ready for their immediate departure. With any luck Zac was still on the roof-garden, she thought as she raced along to his study and scooted across to his desk to search for her and Aimee's passports. One thing was certain, after her humiliating capitulation in his bed she could not risk remaining in Monaco for another night.

'Looking for something?' His lazy drawl brought her head up and she blushed and jumped guiltily away from the desk to find him standing in the doorway.

'Passports,' she replied, swallowing at the sight of him in chinos and a cream shirt, open at the neck to reveal the tanned column of his throat.

'Aimee and I are leaving. I refuse to stay here and be subjected to your vile accusations any more,' she said heatedly.

'Ah.' He stepped into the room and her heart lurched when he shut the door behind him and turned the key in the lock.

She could not look at him without remembering how she had writhed beneath him in abject surrender just hours before and she gave a silent groan of despair as her body stirred into instant life. Her palms felt suddenly damp and she wiped them down her skirt. 'Elise said you wanted to see me about something,' she muttered, tension prickling her skin when he moved towards her. As he walked around his desk she edged away from him, and at his terse command to sit down she subsided into the chair facing him.

He studied her speculatively for a few moments, but his gaze did not quite meet hers and she gained the curious impression that he felt awkward.

'I owe you an apology,' he said brusquely.

Astounded, she stared at him, wondering if she had heard him correctly. Zac apologising to her had to be a first, but the fact that he felt the need to made her realise how much he obviously regretted making love to her. 'It's all right,' she mumbled as she inspected her lap with sudden fascination. 'I'm not proud of my behaviour either. We just got carried away, but obviously it's an experience neither of us wants to repeat.'

Black eyebrows winged upwards. 'I was not apologising for last night, *chérie*,' he said silkily, his eyes glinting with amusement. 'It was an incredible experience that I have every intention of repeating. You enjoyed it too,' he added before she could comment, 'so don't play the innocent martyr with me because you're a wildcat in bed and I have the scratches on my back to prove it.'

'Oh!' Scarlet-faced, she wished a hole would open up and swallow her, and more than anything she longed to wipe his smug grin from his face.

'My only regret about last night is that I was rough with you,' he continued, his husky, accented voice sliding over her like a velvet cloak. 'I was, as you so succinctly put it, carried away, and I'm afraid that in my urgency to possess you I might have hurt you. Did I, *ma petite*?'

His words evoked a stark image in Freya's mind of how she had begged him to take her; how she had enticed him with her desperate pleas to move faster and thrust deeper into her as he took her to the heights of sexual ecstasy. Zac's regrets had nothing on hers, she thought sickly, tearing her gaze from the knowing gleam in his. 'No,' she choked thickly, 'you didn't hurt me, but last night was a mistake I regret bitterly.'

She ran a shaky hand through her hair and forced herself to look at him. 'If it wasn't…that, then what are you apologising for?'

In reply he took a folded document from the drawer and handed it to her. For a few seconds Freya's heart stopped beating and then started again at twice its normal rate. She knew instinctively that it was the results of the paternity test and she stared at him without opening it. 'I already know what it says,' she told him quietly. 'And now, so do you.'

She searched his face for some sign that would tell her how he felt about learning that

Aimee was his child, but his expression was shuttered. This should be her moment of triumph, but she felt empty inside. For two years she'd played out a stupid daydream in her head that one day he would discover he was Aimee's father and would immediately beg her to forgive him for the way he had treated her, before sweeping her into his arms and pleading for a chance for them to live together as a family—in true happy-ever-after tradition. His grim face shattered her dream and the little seed of hope she'd carried in her heart withered and died. He didn't want their child any more than he wanted her, and it was about time she accepted that fact.

'Damn you, Zac,' she burst out when his silence became intolerable. 'There's no need to look so horrified,' she muttered bitterly. 'I don't want a penny of your wretched money. All I ever wanted was for Aimee to have a daddy who would love and protect her, and that clearly isn't going to be you. But I can do those things. I'll be a mother and a father to her and right now I'm taking her home.' She glared at him, and a frisson of unease ran the length of her spine when he stood up and strode around the desk.

'No, *chérie*, you are not,' he said steadily, his eyes narrowing when she jumped up and backed away from him. He could see the hurt and confusion in her eyes and felt a flicker of remorse. But when he closed the gap between them and noted how her pulse was jerking frantically at the base of her throat, he felt a surge of quiet satisfaction. Sexual alchemy was a potent force that held her in its thrall, however much she might resent its power.

There was no point in denying that he was deeply shocked by the results of the paternity test. Aimee was his child, a Deverell who, like him, was a possible carrier of the gene that had caused the illness and deaths of his baby sisters. His one relief was that Aimee was eighteen months old and safe from the risk of developing the disease, which caused death in infants usually before they were a year old.

Discovering that he was a father was something he hadn't been prepared for, but he had felt protective of Freya's child from the moment

Joyce Addison had abandoned her to his care and he knew without doubt that he would love Aimee unconditionally for the rest of his life. Aimee was adorable and, having missed the first eighteen months of her life, he was determined not to miss another day.

His feelings towards Freya were more complicated. On the few occasions that she had crept into his mind during the past two years, he had angrily dismissed her, reminding himself of her true colours. But the moment he had seen her again he'd been forced to accept that his desire for her was as fierce as it had been in the past. He had made love to her last night because he couldn't resist her, and now it seemed that he didn't have to try. She hadn't lied to him, she was the mother of his child and she wanted him with the same urgency that he wanted her. All he had to do now was persuade her to resume her place in his bed.

'It seems that I am one of the rare cases for whom the vasectomy reversed, but now I know Aimee is my child and I accept that I have a responsibility for her.' he began, but Freya interrupted him.

'No, you don't.' She shook her head fiercely, hating the fact that he felt a duty towards Aimee. Her grandmother had tolerated her out of a sense of duty, but it had been a loveless upbringing and she would do everything in her power to prevent her daughter from feeling the same sense of worthlessness that she had felt as a child. 'I hereby absolve you of all responsibility. What were you planning to do, Zac—appease your conscience by arranging regular maintenance payments and maybe send her a birthday card once a year?' she demanded sarcastically. 'Aimee's conception was the result of a freak chance, it wasn't your fault and there's no reason for you to feel obligated towards either of us.'

'It's not a question of obligation,' Zac said forcefully. 'I want to play an active role in my daughter's life.' The ring of steely determination in his voice caused Freya's heart to jerk in her chest and she stared at him, bemused by his unexpected statement.

'You mean you want to arrange visitation rights? Think carefully, Zac. A child is for life, not just for Christmas,' she said sharply. 'It's all very well for you to decide you want to see Aimee occasionally, but what happens when the novelty of fatherhood wears off? I remember how excited I used to feel when my mother promised to visit, and the crushing sense of disappointment when she let me down yet again. I won't allow you to do that to Aimee.'

'That's not how it will be,' he stated angrily. 'Aimee is my child, a Deverell, and I want her to live here in Monaco.'

'But how would that work?' Freya argued faintly, her mind reeling. 'Even if I finish my degree, I'm not sufficiently fluent in French to find a job that would pay rent on a property here. Aimee's home is in England and that's where I'm taking her. If you're serious about wanting a relationship with her, you can easily afford to visit as often as it suits you.' Her tone plainly indicated that she believed he would soon lose interest in playing daddy, and Zac's jaw hardened.

'I wasn't suggesting that we live in separate homes and pass our daughter between us like a parcel. A child needs two parents and I want you and Aimee to move into the penthouse with me.'

For the sum total of twenty seconds Freya experienced a surge of incandescent joy—quickly followed by the feeling that her heart was plummeting towards her toes with the speed of an express elevator. Of course he wanted her to move back in with him—it would be much more convenient for him than having to travel back to England to visit Aimee. She was still stunned by Zac's declaration that he intended to be a proper father. Undoubtedly Aimee would benefit from having both her parents around, but what role was he expecting *her* to play in his life?

'Won't that cramp your style?' she queried sarcastically. 'You can hardly maintain your reputation as Monaco's most eligible bachelor with an ex-lover and a baby in tow.'

His slow, sensual smile sent a tremor of awareness through her. 'Since last night, you're no longer an *ex*-lover, are you?' he murmured softly, his warm breath fanning her ear.

Freya suddenly became aware that he was too close; she could feel the heat from his body and the waves of sexual energy emanating from him triggered alarm bells in her head. She took a jerky step backwards, but his arm snaked around her waist to draw her inexorably towards him.

'You know how it was between us, Freya. Don't deny it,' he said fiercely when she opened her mouth to remonstrate. 'The passion we shared was explosive for both of us, *chérie.*'

'No.' Freya made an inarticulate sound low in her throat as she watched his head descend. Any second now his mouth would touch hers and she would be lost to the simmering, burning need that only Zac could arouse. Outrage battled with desire and won by a narrow margin. 'Do you honestly think you can click your fingers and I'll fall into your arms?' she demanded, shamefully aware that she had done exactly that the previous night. 'Yesterday I was a common slut with a predilection for wealthy lovers—'

'That was before I knew the truth,' he interrupted harshly. 'I know now that I was wrong and I am willing to accept that you didn't sleep with Brooks.'

'That's big of you,' Freya muttered bitterly, 'but you're too late, Zac. It's a pity you didn't believe me two years ago—when I needed you.

Instead you almost destroyed me with your distrust, and, to be frank, I wouldn't come back to you if you were the last man on the planet.'

His slow smile disarmed her and she missed the warning gleam of battle in his eyes. 'We'll see, shall we?' he said softly, tightening his arm around her until her face was pressed against his chest.

'Let go of me, you…brute.' She hammered her fists on his shoulders, like a wild bird frantically beating its wings against the bars of a cage, but he ignored her blows and threaded his other hand through her hair, tilting her face to his. The scorching heat in his gaze sent a quiver of excitement through her and she gave a silent groan of despair. How could she fight him when this was the only place she wanted to be? Clutching the remnants of her pride, she tried to turn her head, but lean fingers held her chin as he angled her mouth to his satisfaction before claiming it with his own in a searing kiss that drove all thoughts of resistance from her mind.

His tongue explored the contours of her lips, stroking, caressing, until he judged the moment she relaxed her guard and thrust into the moist warmth of her mouth in a flagrantly erotic gesture. Freya felt the drugging sweetness of desire flood through her veins, leaving her limp and boneless with longing. Her fists unfurled and she laid her hands flat against his chest, feeling the erratic thud of his heart beneath her fingertips.

'Last night was a mistake. We can't simply take up where we left off two years ago,' she protested when he eased the pressure of his mouth and traced her swollen lips with the tip of his tongue. 'Too much has happened, Zac. You hurt me so badly,' she whispered as she relived the agony of his rejection and the countless nights when she had cried herself to sleep. She was appalled by her weakness—how could she be such a pushover? He was probably congratulating himself that he had demolished her resistance with one kiss, but when she stared into his eyes and saw the undisguised hunger flare in his blue depths she felt a heady sense of elation. He felt it too, this pagan drumbeat of desire that pounded in her veins until she was conscious of nothing but the desperate, over-whelming need to surrender her soul to passion.

'Then let me try to make amends,' he growled against her throat. 'Let me remind you of how good it was between us and show you how good it can be again. We always communicated better without words, *cherie*.' He slid his hands down and curled them possessively around her buttocks, drawing her up against him so that her pelvis was in direct contact with the throbbing force of his arousal.

Freya gasped and he captured the faint sound, grinding his lips on hers with a primitive passion that whipped her senses into a feverish state of anticipation. She was on fire for him and nothing else mattered—not the past and all the pain he'd caused her and not the future and all its uncertainties. She wanted him now, the only man she had ever loved, and when he lifted her into his arms she clung to him, her fingers tearing at his shirt buttons until she was able to part the material and run her hands over the dark hairs that covered his chest.

Zac cleared the surface of his desk with one sweep of his arm before laying her down on the polished wood and immediately covering her body with his own. He deftly removed her blouse and muttered his satisfaction that she wasn't wearing a bra, his voice hoarse as he bent his head and captured the tip of one pink nipple between his lips. The effect on Freya was electric and she arched her back so that her breasts thrust provocatively towards him, the taut, swollen peaks begging for his possession.

She was shaking—or was it him? she wondered feverishly as she pushed his shirt over his shoulders and ran her hands over his smooth, tanned skin. This was madness but they were both caught up in the conflagration that threatened to consume them in a flame of white-hot need. With a rough, almost violent movement he grabbed the hem of her skirt and jerked it up to her waist before skimming his hand over the sensitive flesh of her inner thighs.

'Zac.' His name escaped her lips as a plea rather than a protest. She lifted her hips and he dragged her knickers down before spreading her legs with a deliberate intent that made her tremble with anticipation. When he touched her she thrust against his hand and moaned when his skilful fingers slid into her and began to explore her with a thoroughness that made her clench her teeth as her pleasure built. Through heavy lids she watched his hand move to the zip of his trousers, no thought in her head other than that he should hurry before she died with the urgent need to feel the full length of him inside her.

'You see, Freya, some things never change,' he groaned as he came down on top of her, supporting his weight on his elbows so that the rigid strength of his penis pushed intimately against her eager body. He slid his hand beneath her bottom to lift her towards him, but his words penetrated the haze of sexual heat surrounding her and she bunched her hands on his shoulders to hold him back.

Was it the element of satisfaction in his voice that she had capitulated so easily—yet again? Or was it his arrogant assumption that nothing had changed and she was still a slave to his touch, despite the way he had treated her? She closed her eyes as a wave of nausea swept over her—how could she be so stupid? Zac hadn't changed—he said he believed that she hadn't had an affair with Simon Brooks, but only because the DNA test proved that Aimee was his child. Two years ago he had been so ready to believe the worst of her and if other issues arose between them in the future she had no faith that he would trust her word above all else.

'You're wrong, Zac,' she whispered fiercely. '*I've* changed. I'm not the pathetic, lovesick girl I once was. You abandoned me when I needed you most, and I had to grow up fast. I won't let you do this to me again,' she muttered, tearing her gaze from him as she fought to control the dictates of her body that *begged* for her to surrender and accept his full possession. From somewhere she found the strength to push against his chest, but the glitter in his eyes warned her that she was too late. His body was primed and ready to take her, his breath coming in harsh gasps as he fought for control.

The discreet knock on the study door shattered the tension and the butler, Laurent's, imperturbable tones sounded through the wood. 'Madame Deverell has arrived and is waiting in the salon.'

Hysterical laughter bubbled in Freya's throat. *'Madame?* You have a *wife*?'

'Non, I have a mother—who has impeccable timing,' Zac replied sardonically as he rolled off her and snatched up his shirt, muttering a string of profanities beneath his breath. 'But the very fact that you believe I could be married does not say much about your opinion of me, *chérie.'*

'It's an opinion I formed during the time I've spent struggling to bring up our child,' Freya bit back sharply. She couldn't imagine what he must think of her when she was semi-naked and spread-eagled across his desk. Scarlet-cheeked, she tugged her skirt down and hopped inelegantly from foot to foot trying to pull her knickers on, praying that Zac's mother wouldn't walk in. She'd suffered enough humiliation to last her a lifetime—much of it self-induced, she thought miserably as she recalled her shameless response to him. One thing was clear: she dared not trust herself to be near him for another day. He could deal with his mother and explain why his elegant bachelor pad was littered with toys and teddies, while she collected Aimee and made her escape.

'I'll go and speak to my mother while you tidy yourself up,' he said tersely, his expression unfathomable as he inspected her dishevelled appearance and hot face. He on the other hand looked as cool as a cucumber and had obviously had no difficulty in bringing his desire under control. Any minute now and he would pop a couple of bank notes down her blouse in payment for services rendered, Freya thought furiously, shrivelling beneath his look of haughty disdain. She held her breath until he left the room, and as soon as he had gone raced around his desk and searched for the passports. Flights back to England would stretch her overdraft to its limit, she acknowledged ruefully, but it couldn't be helped, she had to get away.

Ignoring the sound of voices from the sitting room, she raced along the hall to the nursery and snatched up the holdall she'd packed with Aimee's things. With any luck she could collect her daughter from the roof-garden, bid a quick farewell to Jean Lewis and disappear before Zac realised that she had no intention of remaining at the penthouse until he grew bored of fatherhood. At the doorway she spun round and gave one final glance around the room, groaning when she spied Aimee's favourite toy rabbit at the end of the cot. With a muttered curse she dropped the holdall and flew across the carpet to retrieve the toy, her heart sinking at the sound of Zac's voice.

'There you are—I thought you were going to come and meet my mother,' Zac drawled, his eyes narrowing when Freya gasped at the sight of him.

'I…thought Aimee was here,' she said quickly, praying that he wouldn't notice the holdall behind the door.

'She's with Jean in the salon. My mother would very much like to meet you,' he added quietly.

'You never introduced me to her during the time I lived with you,' Freya muttered, remembering how hurt she'd felt when Zac had used to visit Yvette Deverell but never suggested that she accompany him. 'Why the sudden urgency?'

'The situation is different now.' He paused and then explained, 'When you lived here, my mother was still devastated at the loss of my father. She became a virtual recluse and I was the only person she wanted to see. Thankfully she is much better now and she's eager to meet you.'

The glint in Zac's eyes warned Freya that she had no option but to comply and she hastily shoved the passports behind her back and followed him down the hall. Voices were audible from the salon, Jean Lewis' calm tones and another, heavily accented voice, mingled with Aimee's gurgling laughter. 'What an adorable child—how old is she?'

'Eighteen months,' Zac answered his mother's query as he ushered Freya into the room while Jean quietly excused herself. '*Maman,* this is Freya Addison—Aimee's mother.'

'Mademoiselle Addison.' Yvette Deverell stood and held out one elegantly manicured hand to Freya. She was tall, willowy and effortlessly chic in an exquisite dress and jacket from one of the leading fashion houses. Freya immediately felt conscious of the creases in her cheap skirt and, as had so often happened during her childhood, she was swamped by a feeling of inadequacy, not helped when Yvette continued to study her from beneath faintly arched eyebrows, in a silence that spoke volumes. 'You have a delightful little girl,' she commented at last, and Freya stiffened when Zac placed his arm around her waist and drew her forwards.

'Aimee is my daughter, *Maman*.' He spoke softly to his mother. 'You have a granddaughter.'

Freya was prepared for Yvette to look surprised, shocked even, but the expression of horrified dismay on the Frenchwoman's face filled her with cold fury. Suddenly she was eight years old, walking up the path of Nana Joyce's house clutching the hand of the social worker who had collected her from the foster family she had been staying with. There had been no look of pleasure on her grandmother's face when she had opened the door, no welcoming smile.

'You'd better go up to your room, Freya, and mind you don't make any noise. You can come down at teatime as long as you're quiet—I don't expect to be disturbed by childish chatter,' Joyce Addison had greeted her coldly.

To this day she rarely spoke unless spoken to, and even in her own flat she'd crept about on tiptoe out of habit, Freya thought bleakly. Her grandmother had crushed her spirit and destroyed her self-confidence—she would not allow Zac's mother to do the same to Aimee.

'I don't understand. How can this be?' Yvette Deverell was staring at her son, a look of blank incomprehension on her face. 'Are you certain this is your child?'

Her comments were the last straw, Freya decided furiously, her face burning with mortification as she tugged out of Zac's hold and grasped Aimee's hand. It was bad enough that Zac had doubted Aimee's paternity—how dared his mother do the same? 'There was some debate over whether Aimee belonged to the tinker, the tailor or the candlestick maker,' she snapped, her eyes flashing fire as she met Yvette Deverell's stunned glance. 'Zac is Aimee's biological parent, but that's where his involvement ends. Please don't worry, *madame*, I'm taking my daughter home to England and, I assure you, you won't see either of us again.'

'Zac! I don't understand.' Yvette bombarded her son in a torrent of rapid French while Freya spun on her heel and raced towards the door, tugging Aimee after her. But Zac beat her to it and stood blocking her path, his eyes focused intently on her face.

'Let me go,' she said in a low voice that shook as she struggled to keep her emotions in check. 'Aimee doesn't belong here. Your mother just made that abundantly clear. She's my daughter and I'm taking her home.'

'Zac, I insist you tell me what is happening,' Yvette demanded plaintively.

'Calm down, *Maman*,' he ordered impatiently as he lifted Aimee against his chest. Without giving Freya a chance to react, he captured her chin with his lean fingers and lowered his head to take her mouth in a brief, searing kiss. 'There has been a simple misunderstanding, but it's sorted now,' he said coolly, his bruising grip on her chin preventing her from speaking while his eyes burned into hers. 'Freya agrees that our daughter should grow up in Monaco with her family, and from now on she and Aimee will live permanently here in the penthouse with me. Isn't that so, *chérie*?'

CHAPTER SEVEN

'I CAN'T believe you said that to your mother.'
Freya yelled at Zac as she stormed down the hall
after him and followed him into his room. 'I can
see we're going to have to come to some sort of arrangement so that you can see Aimee regularly—
now that you're suddenly determined to win the
award for Father of the Year,' she added sarcastically. 'But I'm not moving into the penthouse just
for your convenience. I do have a life of my own,
you know,' she said sharply, her temper rising when
he ignored her. Breathing hard, she glared at him,
her brain barely registering the fact that he was un-
buttoning his shirt. 'Why are you doing this?' she
demanded angrily. 'You don't want me living here
as some sort of permanent house guest any more
than you want the responsibilities of a child.

'Let me take Aimee home and I swear I'll never contact you again. I don't need you, Zac,' she said thickly, knowing that the words were a lie. She needed him in the same way that she needed oxygen to breathe, but she wouldn't allow her daughter to grow up feeling that she was an encumbrance in her father's life. Aimee was already forming an emotional attachment to Zac and Freya couldn't bear to see him hurt her with his indifference.

'Perhaps you don't, but what about Aimee's needs?' Zac asked quietly. He deciphered the jumble of emotions on her face and felt a curious pain in his gut. After the way he had misjudged her, he supposed she had every right to mistrust his motives, but he didn't like it. 'My mother was shocked to discover that she has a granddaughter,' he said, attempting to explain Yvette Deverell's reaction to Aimee, 'understandably so when she believed I would never have a child.'

'You didn't want a child,' Freya pointed out sharply.

'*Non*, but there were reasons...'

'You mean the idea of fatherhood didn't mix

with your life as a jet-setting playboy,' she agreed scathingly. 'Aimee isn't an accessory that you can pick up or set down when it suits you. She deserves to be loved.'

'And I will love her—I already do,' he vowed, his voice suddenly fierce. 'I can provide her with everything she needs. I regret missing the first eighteen months of her life more than you will ever know and I will not miss another day. I don't want to fight you, Freya—you're her mother and she needs you, but she needs me too and I'll fight through the courts if necessary to keep her here.'

The floor swayed beneath Freya's feet and all colour leached from her face. 'You can't be serious.'

'I've never been more serious in my life,' Zac assured her grimly.

Freya shook her head, feeling as though it were going to explode. She had assumed that Zac would want as little contact as possible with his daughter and she could barely comprehend that he was prepared to fight a custody battle over her. And it was a battle he would surely win, she thought sickly. He could afford the best legal representation, who would argue that Aimee would want for nothing in his care.

What could she offer in comparison? she brooded miserably, thinking of the life they led in England and her daily struggle to hold down a job and look after Aimee properly. Aimee would undoubtedly have a better life here in Monaco, but Zac couldn't seriously expect her to put her life on hold and move in with him, could he?

'I can understand that you want to build a relationship with Aimee and it would be in her best interest if you decide to be a proper father to her. But what role are you expecting me to play in your life?' Freya's voice faltered as she finally registered that he had removed his shirt and was in the process of unzipping his trousers.

'I would have thought that was obvious,' he drawled, trailing his eyes over her flushed face. 'You will resume your role as my mistress. We've already proved that, on a physical level, we're made for each other,' he continued, overriding her gasp of outraged denial. 'The sexual attraction between us is as explosive now as it was two years ago. I know now that you didn't have an affair with Brooks and I can see no reason why I shouldn't take you back in my bed.' His trousers slid to the floor and he stepped out of them before strolling across the room towards her. 'Obviously providing Aimee with a secure and stable upbringing is our main concern and the fact that we can enjoy a fantastic sex life is a bonus, wouldn't you say, *chérie*?'

Despite her fury at his arrogant assumption that she would gratefully accept his offer to grace his bed once more, Freya could not prevent her eyes from straying down to his boxers and her stomach tightened at the burgeoning proof of his arousal jutting unashamedly beneath the black silk. 'You've got a nerve, Zac,' she muttered, licking her suddenly dry lips. 'Clearly, in your belief that you're God's gift, it hasn't occurred to you that I don't want to be your mistress. The idea is ridiculous. We're totally incompatible. Zac! What are you doing?' The last came out as a breathless gasp as he deftly shrugged out of his underwear.

'Taking a shower—I didn't have time earlier after my swim. Come and join me while we finish this fascinating conversation,' he invited with a wolfish smile. His eyes gleamed from beneath heavy lids and the room suddenly throbbed with sexual tension that sent Freya scooting towards the door.

'You must be joking,' she choked, but her words were muffled against his shoulder as he swept her up into his arms as if she were a rag doll and strode purposefully into the *en suite*. 'Zac, we'll talk later... What is the point in this?' she demanded when he activated the shower and stepped beneath the spray with her, still fully clothed and wriggling like an eel to escape him.

'The point, my little vixen,' he said as he trapped her flailing hands in one of his to prevent her raining blows on his chest, 'is to prove that in certain areas, at least, we are completely compatible.' His head descended and he claimed her mouth, silencing her furious words by kissing her into submission. He knew just how to please her, and he felt a jolt of satisfaction when the tight line of her lips suddenly parted and he was able to dip his tongue between them to explore the moist warmth of her mouth.

Freya gave a helpless groan of protest that was lost beneath the pressure of his lips. Her body was still agonisingly aroused from earlier, when he had laid her across his desk. It had taken all her will-power to stop him from taking her and her senses were greedily snatching this second chance for fulfilment. The powerful spray had already soaked through her clothes and, without lifting his mouth from hers, Zac stripped her of her blouse and skirt. Only then did he trail his lips down her throat to her breasts, where he paused and flicked his tongue back and forth across one tight nipple and then the other until she cried out and felt a sharp tug of desire deep in her pelvis. She clung to his shoulders when he knelt before her and drew her knickers down. Water ran down his face and made his skin glisten and the sight of his dark head moving inexorably down to the triangle of blonde curls between her thighs filled her with a frantic sense of urgency that destroyed any thoughts she'd had of denying him.

'Lift your leg,' he growled, his voice thick and slurred with sexual promise as he pushed her gently up against the tiled shower wall and hooked her ankle over his shoulder. Now she was spread before him and he tenderly parted her with his long, clever fingers before dipping his tongue between the velvet folds of her femininity.

Freya gave a muffled sob and dug her fingers into his hair as he explored her with a wicked intimacy that sent quivers of pleasure through her, building higher and higher until she was trembling with need. 'Please, Zac…' she implored him, but he ignored her and flicked his tongue over her clitoris in fierce, fast little movements that tipped her over the edge of ecstasy. She shuddered as her muscles clenched in wave after wave of exquisite sensation and in the throes of her climax he stood, lifted her into his arms and ordered her to wrap her thighs around him. Freya complied instantly, aware of nothing but the dictates of her body that still wanted more, and she closed her eyes on a shocked gasp when he penetrated her with one hard thrust.

Last night he had been so blown away by her eager response to him that he had almost lost control, but this time Zac was determined to prove that he was her master. He cupped her bottom and drove into her with slow, steady strokes that filled her and made her arch her back as her pleasure built again. It was deeper this time, even more intense, and she clung to him, totally enslaved by his domination as he finally gave in to her desperate pleas and increased his pace, taking her hard and fast until she threw back her head and convulsed around him in an orgasm that shattered all her preconceived notions of sexual ecstasy.

Freya sobbed his name and locked her ankles tightly around his back, but, instead of taking his own pleasure, he abruptly withdrew from her and set her back on her feet, his nostrils flaring as he fought for control.

'Why…?' She tailed to a halt and looked at him with a mixture of confusion and scalding embarrassment as she recalled her shameless response to him. Once again she'd proved that she was completely in his power and she knew he would ruthlessly use that knowledge to bend her to his will.

'I don't keep condoms in the shower,' he told

her bluntly, his eyes trailing over her scarlet cheeks. 'Remiss of me—I must remember in future that you enjoy sex outside the bedroom as much as in it.' His eyes glinted with amusement at her outraged glare and, before she could argue, he took the bar of soap and began to stroke it in circular movements over her breasts. 'Now I know that the vasectomy reversed I can't risk another accidental conception.'

'Aimee may have been an accident, but I don't regret having her,' Freya said heatedly, a shudder running through her when he slid the bar of soap over her stomach and lower to her thighs and buttocks. 'That'll do, I'm clean enough,' she said, bitterly resenting the way her body was quivering in anticipation of his touch once more. Clearly she was some sort of nymphomaniac, she thought grimly, because she couldn't get enough of him.

'Be honest, Zac, you never wanted children. You wouldn't have had a vasectomy if you had. You can still have a relationship with Aimee if I take her back to England,' she told him when he stepped out of the shower, wrapped a towel around her and carried her into his bedroom, 'but you don't really want to be tied down with a child living permanently here in the penthouse.' Her breath left her body on a gasp when he dropped her unceremoniously on the bed, but to her disappointment he did not join her and instead crossed to his wardrobe and selected a clean shirt and trousers.

'Aimee is my daughter and she belongs here,' he said as he slid into his clothes with his usual lithe grace. 'You know from your own childhood experiences that it's best for a child to grow up in a stable environment with two parents and, for that reason, I'm prepared to allow you back in my life.'

He slid his arms into his suit jacket and strolled over to the bed, his mouth curving into a mocking smile as he stared down at her lying sprawled on the silk bedspread. 'I have to go to the office for a couple of hours but I'll keep the image in my mind of your delectable naked body spread across my bed. This is where you belong, *chérie*, ready and willing to please me.' He leaned over her and stemmed her furious rebuttal of his arrogant statement by kissing her senseless before he straightened and traced his thumb pad over her swollen lips. 'You want me, Freya, and as my mistress you can have me, every single night. Now, be a good girl and stop arguing. Most women would be grateful for the opportunity to move in with a billionaire lover.'

Good girl! Incandescent with rage, Freya wondered if she could beat him to death with a pillow. 'Unluckily for you, I'm not most women, and if you think I'd ever agree to be your grateful, *obedient* mistress you're going to be disappointed,' she hissed between her clenched teeth.

Zac was already at the door, but he paused and turned to give her a wicked grin. 'Good—I'd much rather have a disobedient mistress,' he drawled. 'It promises to be a lot more fun.'

Two weeks later Freya sat gloomily on a sun lounger, aware that even the beauty of her surroundings failed to lighten her mood. The penthouse roof-garden was a suntrap where scarlet geraniums grew in profusion, their bold colour vying for attention with the azure pool and the sea sparkling on the horizon. She had spent the morning watching while Aimee played with her father in the pool, but now Jean had taken the little girl to the nursery for a nap and she and Zac were alone.

'Are you hot? Come for a swim to cool off,' Zac invited, his eyes gleaming with wicked amusement when she quickly shook her head. 'I promise I won't duck you.'

'Your promises count for nothing,' Freya told him firmly, dragging her gaze from the sight of him floating on his back in the pool. His skin had darkened to bronze in the hot sun and she felt the familiar weakness in the pit of her stomach when he swam to the steps and hauled himself out. Droplets of water trickled down his chest and clung to the mass of wiry black hairs that arrowed down beneath the waistband of his swimming shorts. The muscles of his taut abdomen were clearly visible beneath his skin and when he walked over to her and picked up a towel Freya suddenly became fascinated with the view over the bay.

'You practically drowned me the last time you

persuaded me to swim with you,' she accused, recalling how he had swum up behind her and tugged her under. Taken by surprise, she'd been forced to cling to him—out of her depth in more ways than one, she acknowledged ruefully as the memory of being clamped against his muscular chest while he carried her to the edge of the pool filled her mind.

'Don't you trust me?' He grinned unrepentantly, but beneath his teasing tone she caught a hint of seriousness and she bit her lip as she silently debated the question.

Did she trust him? As far as their child was concerned, she did not doubt that he would always consider Aimee's welfare paramount. Two weeks had passed since he had received the results of the DNA test and stated his intention to be a proper father to his daughter, and in that time he had proved himself to be a devoted parent. Freya knew that the bond between father and daughter was already so strong that she could never break it.

Aimee adored her *papa* and with each day that passed Freya felt more and more trapped. She loved her daughter and wanted what was best for her, and undoubtedly Aimee was thriving here in Monaco, showered in affection from Zac, her nanny, Jean Lewis, and the other members of the penthouse staff. Even the taciturn butler, Laurent, had been won over by the baby and could often be found padding up and down the hall on his hands and knees while Aimee gleefully balanced on his back.

Aimee was enjoying the happy family life that Freya had dreamed of as a child, but it was Zac's mother who had surprised her the most. Yvette Deverell seemed utterly entranced with her little granddaughter and was the most loving, devoted grandmother imaginable. She visited most days and Freya was still amazed by the sight of the elegant Frenchwoman sitting cross-legged on the carpet playing tea parties with Aimee and her teddies. Aimee had formed a very special relationship with *Mamie*, which Freya would never try to destroy. Her daughter belonged here—but what about her? Where did she belong? she wondered bleakly.

Zac had told her that he wanted her to move

in with him for Aimee's sake, but since then he'd made no further reference to her becoming his mistress, or how he envisaged their future together—possibly because he had now decided that they didn't have one, she brooded dismally. He had made no attempt to make love to her during the past two weeks even though he knew full well that she would not resist him. Perhaps he had found her eagerness unattractive, she thought on a wave of embarrassment, or maybe, now that he'd had her, he was already tired of her. Whatever his reasons, he had spent the past weeks being charmingly attentive each evening when he returned home from work, but conspicuously absent from her bed each night, and she felt confused and, if she was honest, incredibly frustrated.

She tried not to look at him rubbing the towel over his damp body, but she was painfully aware of the fact that his wet shorts were clinging to his thighs, leaving little to her imagination. Hopefully he would announce that he had some work to do in his study. It was Saturday, and she remembered that when she had lived with him he had spent most of his weekends either working or indulging his passion for a variety of sports, but to her dismay he did not immediately disappear into the penthouse and instead lowered himself into the chair next to hers. She instantly stiffened and her heart began to thud heavily in her chest. He was too close and her senses flared when he idly placed his arm along the back of her chair.

'What are these?' he queried, glancing at the photo albums on the table.

'You said you'd like to see some pictures of Aimee when she was first born,' she replied, grateful for the excuse to edge away from him. 'My neighbour has a key to my flat and I asked her to send these over. They're mainly snaps taken with a disposable camera and the quality isn't brilliant,' she said apologetically as he silently leafed through the album where she had faithfully recorded every milestone of Aimee's development. 'Aimee's a little poseur, don't you think?' She laughed, studying the image of her daughter on her first birthday.

'She's beautiful,' Zac murmured huskily, his accent suddenly very pronounced as he stared at the picture of a smiling Aimee proudly showing off her first tooth. He had missed so much, he acknowledged as he picked up another picture of Aimee as a newborn baby. Someone else had obviously taken the photo of Freya in the delivery room, smiling bravely despite the exhaustion in her eyes as she clutched her tiny bundle.

Freya looked young and scared as she faced the stark reality of coping with motherhood alone, but he recognised the determined set of her chin and felt a flare of admiration for her. Freya's fragile looks were deceptive; she had a backbone of steel and he found himself in awe of her strength. She had stated that she didn't need him and he had no doubts that, if it had not been for the accident, she would have brought Aimee up to be a happy, well-adjusted child without any help from him.

Now he knew Aimee was his child and he was willing to try and atone for misjudging Freya by suggesting that they become lovers once more. He knew without conceit that most women would jump at this chance—but, typically of Freya, she had reacted as though he were asking her to do something unpleasant, he thought irritably. He was offering her a life of luxury that most women would give their eye-teeth for—what more did she want, for heaven's sake?

He wanted things settled between them; he was impatient to bed her—hell, he was practically climbing the walls with sexual frustration—but, taken aback by her violent opposition to his suggestion, he had decided to play it cool and, instead of sweeping her off to bed, he had kept his distance while he waited for her to acknowledge that, on a physical level at least, they were made for each other.

He wanted a warm and willing woman in his bed, not a resentful little shrew, but unfortunately his efforts to charm her had so far been unsuccessful. For a man used to getting his own way instantly, it was hugely frustrating, and he felt curiously tense and unsettled and he was fast running out of patience. Perhaps the time had come for a change of tactics? he brooded. Perhaps he should forget his good intentions and make love to her until she was utterly compliant to the idea of resuming their relationship on his terms?

A loose photo slipped from the back of the album and he reached down to retrieve it at the same moment as Freya. Their hands briefly touched before she snatched her fingers away and she gave an incoherent murmur when he turned the photo over and stared at his own image.

She must have taken it soon after she had moved in with him, he guessed, glancing speculatively at her pink cheeks. Had she kept it because he had meant something to her even though he had done his best to destroy her with his mistrust?

'I didn't know that was in there. I'd forgotten I'd even taken it,' Freya said as she gathered up the rest of the photos and slotted them back into the album. 'I'll get rid of it. It doesn't mean anything to me.' She held out her hand for the picture, praying he wouldn't realise that the edges were furled from where she had held it so often. It would be unbearably humiliating if he should ever guess that she had mooned over his image like a lovesick teenager.

She swallowed when he leaned forwards and placed the photo in her hand, his gaze settling on her hot face. 'We had some good times, didn't we, *chérie*?' he said coolly.

'You mean the sex was good,' she muttered, striving to sound indifferent and aware that her voice was annoyingly breathless. She didn't want to remember the time she'd lived with him; it was too painful, especially now that she was back at the penthouse and Zac was suddenly being so charming. It had been easier when he'd denounced her as a cheating whore—at least then she had been able to kid herself that she hated him.

'It was more than good. There were any number of women I could have had sex with,' he said coolly, the nuance in his tone telling her that those women would have been far more experienced between the sheets than a shy virgin from a sleepy English backwater.

'Well, I don't suppose your bed was empty for very long after you threw me out of it,' Freya said bitterly. 'Annalise Dubois for one was determined to snare you.'

'Perhaps,' he agreed with a shrug. 'I admit I have never lived the life of a monk, either before you were my mistress or after we split up. But I had the best, most unforgettable sex with you, *cherie*.' He suddenly leaned forwards and placed his hands on the arms of her chair, effectively caging her in. His brilliant blue eyes glinted with a message she didn't dare decipher and for the life of her she could not help focusing on his mouth. He was so gorgeous, she thought despairingly. Would she ever be free from this ache that seemed to be a permanent feature in her chest? She could not ignore the unmistakable prickle of sexual energy between them and shrank back in her seat, fighting her body's traitorous response to him and licking her lips nervously when he leaned even closer.

'Even when I despised you, I realised that the sexual chemistry between us burns as strong as before. I know you feel it too. I've seen the way you watch me when you think I'm not looking,' he said bluntly, his gaze trapping hers as if he knew exactly what was going on inside her head.

'You obviously have a vivid imagination,' she snapped, blushing furiously. 'Let me up. I want to go and check on Aimee. She's probably woken from her nap by now.' She tried to push him away but his warm breath fanned her skin and she gave a low moan, half protest and half pleasure, when he brushed his lips lightly over hers. It felt like heaven after the past two weeks when he had made no attempt to entice her into his bed. He had treated her with polite defer-ence, as if she were an honoured guest at the penthouse, but, rather than feeling reassured that he was obviously no longer interested in her, she had *ached* for him to take her in his arms.

Now Freya's lips parted of their own accord. She couldn't help it—he only had to look at her and she was lost, she conceded helplessly. She hated herself for her weakness, but the stroke of his tongue was sweetly beguiling, and when he delved between her lips to explore the moist inner warmth of her mouth she responded with all the pent up need that had kept her awake until dawn every night since she had arrived in Monaco.

Zac's hands remained gripping her chair, his knuckles white with the effort of restraining himself from reaching out to caress her smooth skin—no longer pale, but warmed to the colour of pale gold from the sun. She was so lovely, and he was so very hungry for her, he acknowledged grimly as he felt his body react with shaming eagerness to the feel of her deliciously soft lips parting beneath his. The time for patience was over and he wanted to reacquaint himself with every inch of her delectable body.

He knew she wanted him. He saw it in the way desire darkened her eyes to the colour of a stormy sea and felt it in her unguarded response to him when he kissed her. She belonged with him, in his bed. He had hurt her, and for that he was sorry, but he was a pragmatic man. The tension and mistrust between them was in the past and he could see no reason why they should not enjoy the explosive passion that had always existed between them. But now was not the time, he conceded with a groan.

The scent of her skin was ambrosia and he inhaled sharply, his nostrils flaring as he sought to bring his hormones under control. 'My mother has invited us over—although I believe she used the lure of lunch as an excuse to see her grand-daughter,' he added dryly. 'You'd better go and put some clothes on and dress Aimee in one of the new outfits Yvette bought her.'

He moved abruptly away from her, leaving Freya with the distinct impression that she had been dismissed. But then she had served her purpose, she conceded dismally. It was obvious that Zac had wanted her to agree to take Aimee to his mother's, and kissing her into submission had seemed the simplest method of getting his own way. It was entirely her own fault that she was such a weak, pathetic fool where he was concerned, she told herself sternly as she marched into the penthouse, unaware that he had dived into the pool and was slicing through the water as if his life depended on it.

CHAPTER EIGHT

YVETTE DEVERELL still lived at La Maison des Fleurs, the pretty white-walled villa where Zac had spent his childhood. She greeted Freya warmly and beamed with genuine delight when Aimee held out her arms, demanding to be picked up.

'And how is *mon petit ange* today? Have you come to play with your *mamie*?' she cooed, her elegantly made-up face breaking into a wide smile. 'Freya, Aimee looks adorable in her little dress,' she commented as she led the way outside to the terrace where lunch was to be served. 'The boutique has the same style in blue. I'll buy it for her tomorrow.'

'That's very kind, but she has so many clothes,' Freya murmured, thinking of the numerous exquisite outfits Yvette had already bought Aimee, as well as the stack of toys and teddies that now filled the nursery.

'But I love to buy her things.' Zac's mother's smile faded a little and she glanced worriedly at Freya. 'My heart was so empty after my husband died, but now my granddaughter has filled that space. Perhaps I seem too forward; too eager and you resent my intrusion? But I cannot stop myself from loving her,' she finished, her voice wavering slightly.

Freya thought of her dismal childhood with her own grandmother, whose cold indifference had been so hurtful, and she gave Yvette a smile. 'I don't resent you or your obvious affection for Aimee,' she promised softly. She glanced across the lawn, to where Zac was tickling Aimee and making her squeal with laughter and felt a flutter of fear in her chest. Did she have the right to take Aimee back to England—away from this beautiful place and the people who loved her? 'I'm glad she has a family,' she said quietly. 'She's so happy here.'

Yvette glanced at her speculatively. 'And what about you, Freya?' she enquired gently. 'I hope you are happy too. My son has not confided in me and I would never presume to ask, but I know things have not always been as they should be between you.' She smiled and tentatively touched Freya's hand. 'I would very much like us to be friends.'

Warmth stole through Freya's veins and she returned Yvette's smile. She realised that Zac's mother was probably anxious for them to have a good relationship so that she could continue to see Aimee, but she seemed to be genuinely caring, and after a lifetime of rejection Freya could not help but respond to the Frenchwoman's kindness.

'I'd like that too,' she said, swallowing the sudden lump in her throat. She was glad of the opportunity to establish a relationship with Zac's mother, but there was no escaping the fact that it was time she had a similar conversation with Zac himself. She couldn't remain in Monaco as his guest indefinitely, and she was adamant that she would not accept his outrageous offer to live with him as his mistress, but how were they going to organise parenting Aimee when they lived a thousand miles apart?

Lunch was a relaxed affair during which Yvette regaled Freya with tales of Zac's boyhood and his frequent daring exploits that she laughingly insisted had turned her hair prematurely grey. From the sound of it, Zac had enjoyed a wonderfully happy childhood in the care of his loving parents. Yvette had clearly cherished being a mother and it seemed curious that she had not had more children. Perhaps they had been content, just the three of them, Freya mused enviously. Zac must have been the centre of his parents' world and had grown up confident of their love. She wanted Aimee to grow up in the same environment of happy family life, but the reality was that she was a single mother and she still didn't know exactly how Zac saw his future role in his daughter's life.

'Now, *ma petite*,' Yvette said to Aimee after lunch, 'what shall we do this afternoon, while *Papa* takes your *maman* out on his boat? Would you like to play on your swing?'

Aimee joyfully clapped her hands and scrambled off Freya's lap. She was fascinated by the wooden swing in *Mamie*'s garden and trotted off with her grandmother without a backward glance at Freya.

'I'm not happy about leaving her,' Freya muttered, trying to hide the pang of hurt that her baby seemed perfectly happy without her. 'You go out on the boat; I'd prefer to stay here.'

'She'll be fine for a couple of hours. My mother won't allow her out of her sight for a second,' Zac reassured her. 'I thought you might enjoy a relaxing afternoon,' he added persuasively. 'You must have found it a strain being Aimee's sole carer, but now we can share the responsibility and you can spend some time off duty.'

'I've never minded looking after her,' Freya argued, refusing to admit that there had been times when she'd felt overwhelmed by the enormity of bringing up a child on her own.

'I know, and you've done an amazing job, but I don't underestimate how hard it must have been. You're not alone any longer, Freya, and it's time you accepted that fact.' He paused fractionally and then murmured, 'Besides, it will give us an opportunity to talk. I've a suggestion I want to put to you.'

Freya couldn't help blushing when she recalled his last suggestion—that she should share his bed again. Did he think he stood a better chance of persuading her when he had her trapped on his boat? she wondered grimly. The worst of it was she wasn't at all confident she would be able to resist him if he tried to make love to her again.

But, as usual, Zac was utterly determined to have his own way, she realised bitterly as he steered her through the house and out to his car. Refusing to go with him was pointless; she didn't doubt for a second that he would fling her over his shoulder and carry her onto his boat, and she preferred to keep what little dignity she had left intact.

It was a short drive from La Maison des Fleurs to the marina and her temper at his high-handedness was still simmering when they parked, but as they walked along the quay and she smelled the sea air she could not help but relax a little. She had always loved the sea and her eyes scanned along the line of fabulous yachts and motor cruisers before straying to Zac, who was striding along next to her. In cream chinos and a navy polo shirt he was a tanned, gorgeous, billionaire playboy who turned heads and drew admiring glances wherever he went. Was she mad to have turned down his offer to be his mistress?

The Isis was a stunning looking craft from the outside and inside she was truly sumptuous. As Freya glanced around the luxuriously appointed salon with its champagne coloured leather sofas, and cherry wood fitments, she felt as though she had stepped back in time and was once again the naïve young girl who had worked briefly as Zac's stewardess, before he had enticed her into his bed with his potent, sexy charm. Stifling a sigh, she followed him up on deck and leaned against the boat rail as *The Isis*'s skipper steered smoothly out of the harbour and into the open sea.

'You said you wanted to talk,' she reminded Zac stiffly when he came to stand next to her. He was too close for comfort and she felt her senses flare into urgent life when he lifted his hand and stroked her hair back from her face.

'We need to discuss our future relationship once you've agreed to move permanently into the penthouse,' he agreed in a tone that warned

Freya he intended to lay down the rules and expected her to agree.

'It's going to be a short discussion, then, as we don't have a relationship and I have no intention of moving in with you permanently,' she muttered, and caught her breath at his sudden grin.

'I'm going to have to do something about that sassy tongue of yours,' he threatened softly. He paused and stared at her as if he could not tear his eyes from the delicate beauty of her face. 'I have never felt so alive as when I'm with you, *chérie*,' he admitted, looking faintly stunned by the realisation before he lowered his head and claimed her mouth in a slow, drugging kiss that left Freya breathless and more confused than ever. She loved him and she knew he loved Aimee—wasn't that enough reason to sacrifice her pride and agree to his proposition? she thought dazedly. Shouldn't she sacrifice her own longing to be loved and settle for a life of luxury and amazing sex?

When he finally lifted his head, her lips were stinging and to her shame she realised that she didn't want to talk, she wanted him to sweep her off to his cabin, throw her down on the bed and make love to her with a fierce, primitive passion—giving her no choice in the matter and ignoring all her doubts. 'We'll talk later,' he threatened ominously, the gleam in his cobalt-blue gaze warning her that he knew exactly what he did to her. 'But first we'll swim and lie out in the sun for a while. Aimee will love staying with my mother and we have the whole afternoon to relax and unwind.'

Relax! When he was looking at her with that sensual gleam in his eyes? It seemed unlikely, Freya thought on a wave of panic. 'I didn't bring a swimming costume with me,' she muttered when he finally released her and led her over to a couple of sun loungers arranged on the deck.

'Everything you need is below deck,' Zac assured her. 'Follow me and I'll show you where you can change.'

Zac's taste in swimwear left a lot to be desired, Freya decided later as she cautiously arranged herself on a sun lounger. The minuscule green and gold bikini he'd brought for her was barely decent, just three triangles of material that left a worrying amount of her flesh on display. Not that he had voiced any objections, she mused, a tremor running through her body when he turned his head and she felt his brilliant blue gaze skim over her.

The tension was back, a prickling, tangible force, and all afternoon she had tried to ignore the sexual chemistry that simmered between them, but now, as their eyes clashed, she glimpsed his unconcealed hunger and knew that it mirrored her own.

Damn him, she thought frantically, and damn the dictates of her treacherous body. This was a man who, two years ago, had seduced her into becoming his mistress, but had considered her of so little importance that he hadn't bothered to reveal he had undergone a surgical procedure to ensure he could never father a child. When she had fallen pregnant he had adamantly refused to believe that the child was his. He had torn her heart to shreds with his vile insults, and even now he only accepted that he'd been wrong because of the results of a DNA test, not because he trusted her.

And yet, despite everything he had done to

her, she still wanted him. He was like a fever in her blood and when she was around him nothing else mattered except that he assuage this burning, aching desire that was slowly sending her out of her mind.

Taking a deep breath, she sat up and faced him. All afternoon he had kept their conversation deliberately light, seducing her with his sharp wit so that she had almost kidded herself that they had gone back in time and none of the hurt and pain had ever happened. But she was no longer the impressionable young girl who had hung on his every word. She was a single mother trying to do the best for her child.

'Zac…' She paused fractionally and then said in a low voice, 'It's time I went home.'

'There's no rush,' he replied lazily. 'My mother promised to give Aimee her tea and bath.'

'No. I mean it's time I went back to England— with Aimee. I've had a letter from the yacht club, asking when I'll be returning to work,' she continued when he made no comment, 'and it's only fair that I give them a firm date. They won't keep my job open indefinitely.'

Zac stiffened and swung his legs off his sun lounger so that he was sitting facing her. 'I have never asked about your work before,' he said quietly, forcing himself to ignore his frustration that she seemed hell bent on fighting him, and trying, for the first time, to understand what was going on inside her head. 'Tell me exactly what you do at the yacht club.'

'I'm a receptionist. It's hardly a glittering career, I know,' she muttered defensively when his brows arched, 'but the wages are reasonable and the owners are nice. They've always allowed me to take time off if Aimee is ill. The nursery won't take children if they're unwell,' she explained when he said nothing.

'And this job, it means a lot to you?'

'No, it's just a job—a rather vital commodity for a single mother, wouldn't you say?' she said, feeling the first prickle of unease when he continued to study her speculatively. 'I need to work, Zac.'

'Why?' he demanded with a shrug. 'I realise that in the past it was a necessity, but now I know Aimee is my child and naturally I will support her. How can you even think about taking her away when she is clearly so happy here?' he demanded angrily. 'There's no way I will allow you to unsettle her and force her to live in that *hovel* you euphemistically call home. Apart from anything else, it would break my mother's heart if she were to be separated from her grandchild.'

The desire to point out that she had been forced to live in a *hovel* because of his utter lack of faith in her was so strong that Freya had to bite her lip. There was no point in indulging in a slanging match when what was needed was a calm, rational discussion about their daughter's future. 'I appreciate how much your mother loves Aimee and, believe me, I wouldn't want to do anything to spoil their relationship. But my life is in England.'

'Then go back to England,' Zac growled angrily, 'but you'll go alone. Aimee's life is here now, among her family who love her.'

'Are you saying I don't?' In her agitation, Freya jumped to her feet and glared at him. 'I would lay down my life for her and I will never abandon her the way my mother abandoned me.'

She spun away from him, blinded by her tears, and let out a cry when he grabbed her hand and pulled her down onto his sun lounger. 'Don't,' she pleaded when he leaned over her, his eyes glittering with an intensity that made her heart thud in her chest. 'I understand that you want to be a proper father to Aimee, but I can't leave her here with you, you must see that. We both love her,' she whispered sadly, 'but I don't know how we can ever find a solution that will allow us to both be full-time parents to her.'

'Don't you?' Zac propped himself up on one elbow and trailed his finger lightly down her cheek. 'The solution is obvious, *chérie*. We'll get married.'

'Say that again!' Freya muttered weakly as shock ricocheted through her. For a brief few seconds she was overwhelmed by a sensation of piercingly sweet joy, but already that feeling was fading as common sense kicked in. Zac had asked her to marry him, but she was under no illusion that he was about to profess his undying love for her. And as far as she was concerned, love was the only reason she would contemplate marriage.

'You asked how we could find a solution to the problem of shared parenting of Aimee and I'm simply suggesting that the most obvious answer is for us to get married,' Zac replied in a measured tone, as if he were explaining something to a small child.

'How can a marriage of convenience between two people who actively dislike each other be a solution to anything?' Freya cried. 'I agree that the only reason for us to get married is to provide our daughter with a stable family life and it might possibly work at first, but how do you think Aimee would feel as she grew older and realised that we were only together for her sake? It wouldn't be fair on her, and it wouldn't be fair on us, either. What if you met someone and fell in love?' The idea of him loving another woman when he had never loved her was agonising, but it was a reality she had to accept. 'Or what if I did? We would have to face the agonising decision of whether to put Aimee through a divorce, or whether to sacrifice what could be our one chance of happiness.'

'If we were married I assure you I would remain

faithful,' Zac bit out, his eyes glinting. He was still lying on his side, leaning over her, but she could feel the angry tension that gripped his muscles and acknowledged that now was not a good time to try and ease away from him. Instead she forced herself to lie passively on the sun lounger even though she was acutely conscious of the effect his near-naked body was having on hers.

'I cannot speak for you, of course,' he said stiffly, struggling to disguise his fury that she had obviously contemplated shopping around for another partner. Who was he? Had she already met someone back in England and was hoping that the relationship might become permanent? After the way he had rejected her two years ago, he could hardly blame her, he conceded grimly, but the idea that she could choose to marry another man who would then be Aimee's step-father made him feel physically sick.

'I'm not saying that I have anyone in mind right now,' Freya muttered crossly, fighting the urge to reach up and stroke back the lock of dark hair that had fallen onto his brow. 'But who knows what the future holds? I might meet my soul mate tomorrow and I'd like to have the chance to experience love. My life hasn't been overflowing with it so far,' she added bleakly.

'The love you speak of is the stuff of childish fairy tales,' Zac told her impatiently. 'A successful marriage has its roots in friendship, mutual respect and common goals—in our case the desire to bring our daughter up in a happy family environment.'

'There's more to marriage than a…clinical contract,' Freya argued fiercely.

'You mean passion? I don't foresee any problems on that score, do you, *chérie*?' He moved over her with lightning speed, crushing her beneath him as he claimed her mouth in a statement of pure possession. He forced his tongue between her lips in a flagrantly erotic gesture, probing, exploring, demanding a response that she was unable to deny. One hand tangled in her hair to hold her fast while the other roamed up and down her body, traced the shape of her hip before sliding up to curve around her breast. 'The bedroom is the one place I know our marriage will work,' he growled against her throat, before he moved lower, trailing a line of kisses to the valley between her breasts.

His breath was hot on her skin. She was burning up, Freya thought feverishly, feeling her breasts swell and tighten until they ached for him to caress them. She couldn't think logically and nothing else seemed to matter except that he should continue touching her and kissing her and she made no attempt to stop him when he unfastened the halter straps of her bikini and peeled the material down to expose her breasts to his hungry gaze.

Perhaps she should stop wishing for the moon and settle for what Zac was offering? He might not love her, but he wanted to marry her and from the sound of it he was prepared to be a faithful husband as well as a devoted father to Aimee. Freya caught her breath when he cupped her breast in his palm and lowered his head to stroke his tongue over her nipple. The sensation was so exquisite that she arched towards him, wanting, needing, more of the same and she whimpered softly when he drew the tight peak fully into his mouth.

She loved him so much. He was the only man she would ever love and for her there would never be anyone else, but what about him? What if, despite his good intentions, his desire for her faded and he met someone else? Would he embark on a discreet affair, while maintaining the façade of a happy marriage for Aimee's sake? It would be worse than suffering a slow death, she thought despairingly. She had spent her formative years knowing that she was merely tolerated by her grandmother. The prospect of spending the rest of her life trapped in a loveless marriage was unbearable.

Zac lifted his head from her breast and shifted slightly so that he could feather light kisses down over her flat stomach and a quiver of pure longing flooded through her. The urge to surrender to the desperate need for him to possess her was overwhelming, but she couldn't give in again.

'Do you honestly believe you could experience this level of passion with anyone else, Freya?' he demanded rawly, his eyes burning into hers when he lifted his head and stared down at her.

'Perhaps not, but mind-blowing sex is not a

good enough reason for me to want to marry you, any more than marrying for Aimee's sake,' she said crisply, finally finding the strength to push him away. 'There has to be another way, some sort of compromise where we can both share her and also be free to get on with our own lives.'

Having spent his entire adult life avoiding commitment, Zac made the unwelcome discovery that freedom had suddenly lost its appeal and he hated the idea of Freya *getting on with life* without him. But he recognised the determined set of her chin and grimly conceded that she was the only woman he had ever met whose stubborn streak matched his own. He couldn't frogmarch her up the aisle, and for now he would have to concede a temporary defeat.

She was fumbling with her bikini, her fingers visibly shaking as she dragged the material over her breasts. The hard peaks of her nipples strained against the clingy Lycra and instinct told him that she was fighting her own internal battle. It was tempting to haul her into his arms and prove beyond doubt that the passion they shared was impossible to recreate with anyone else, but he forced himself to move away from her.

'So that's your final answer, is it? You refuse to marry me, but you agree that we need to reach a compromise whereby we can both be involved in Aimee's upbringing.' He sounded indifferent, almost bored, and faintly relieved, Freya thought miserably. In turning him down she had quite possibly made the biggest mistake of her life, but at least she had saved him from a similar fate. 'Just so long as you understand that Aimee will grow up here in Monaco,' he added coolly, a frown crossing his face when a discreet cough alerted him to the presence of the skipper who had emerged from the lower deck.

'I thought the meaning of compromise is to come to a mutual agreement, not for one person to lay down the law,' Freya muttered, but Zac was no longer listening and was already striding along the deck. Her patchy French meant that she had trouble following his conversation with his uniformed crew-member but his body language unsettled her and she quickly stood and thrust her arms into her robe.

'What is it? What's the matter?' she demanded when Zac walked back to her.

He hesitated fractionally and then said, 'My mother has sent a message via the satellite phone saying that Aimee seems unwell. I've instructed Claude to head straight back to port.'

Panic immediately coiled in Freya's stomach. 'How do you mean—unwell? Yvette must have given more details than that.'

'I'm sorry, *chérie*, that's all I know,' Zac said, his voice softening when he saw the flare of anxiety in her eyes. 'We'll be back at La Maison des Fleurs within the hour.' He paused and then murmured, 'It's quite possible that my mother is overreacting. Many years ago she lost two babies in quick succession and she is bound to be ultra-protective of Aimee.'

'How terrible for her.' Freya momentarily forgot her concern for her own baby as she con-templated Yvette Deverell's devastating losses. 'Was that before you were born?'

For a moment it seemed that Zac did not want to answer and his face was shuttered when he glanced at her. '*Non*, I was fourteen—old enough to understand my parents' grief but sadly unable to comfort them, although I did my best.'

'I'm sure you were a great comfort to them.' Freya had a dozen questions she wanted to ask, but it was clear Zac did not want to discuss the tragedy that had blighted his family. He'd said that Yvette had lost her children when they were babies—had they died as a result of cot-death? She had read somewhere that the syndrome could affect more than one sibling and certainly it must have been utterly heartbreaking for Zac and his parents. She could understand now why Yvette adored Aimee, but some maternal sixth sense warned her that Zac's mother wasn't over-reacting. Something was seriously wrong.

The journey back to the port seemed to take for ever and she busied herself by going below deck to change out of her bikini. Her earlier pleasure in the boat trip had evaporated and she wished she had never allowed Zac to persuade her to leave Aimee. She felt guilt-ridden that she had abandoned her baby even for a couple of hours, especially as it had resulted in her and Zac being at loggerheads once more. Her daughter was the only important person in her life, she reminded herself fiercely, and everyone else, including Zac, took second place.

The moment the car drew up outside La Maison des Fleurs, Freya flew through the front door and skidded to a halt when Yvette hurried forwards to greet them. 'How is Aimee?' she asked urgently, fear seizing her when she stared at the Frenchwoman's worried expression.

'Not good, I'm afraid,' Yvette replied shakily, turning her gaze from Freya to Zac. 'Thank God you're here. The doctor is with Aimee now and he says she must go straight to the hospital.'

With a muffled cry Freya shot past Zac's mother, into the sitting room where Aimee was lying, pale and seemingly lifeless on the sofa.

'Aimee, Aimee! What's wrong with her?' she beseeched the doctor who was standing, grave-faced, close to the child. She could hear Zac urgently asking his mother when Aimee had first shown signs of being ill, and Yvette's explanation that the toddler had seemed tired after playing on the swing.

'I was surprised because I know she usually

has a nap in the morning, but I made her a bed on the sofa and thought she would sleep for a little while. After two hours I was beginning to feel anxious,' Yvette said tearfully. 'I was relieved when she stirred, but almost immediately she was sick and when I drew back the blinds she screamed as if the light hurt her eyes. Since then she has been as you see her now. The doctor has confirmed she is running a high temperature but her symptoms could mean many things...' Yvette broke off helplessly and Freya swung round to the doctor.

'What do you think is wrong with her?'

'I can't say for sure but she is showing classic symptoms of meningitis,' he said quietly. 'It's best that she goes to the hospital where tests will confirm the diagnosis. I think the ambulance is here now.' He took one look at Freya's ashen face and patted her arm. 'Try not to worry, *madame*, your daughter will be in good hands.'

Meningitis—the word sounded over and over in Freya's head as the ambulance hurtled through the traffic. It was every parent's worst nightmare, renowned for striking without warning and with potentially fatal results. Aimee's life could not be in danger; she frantically sought to reassure herself, but when she stared at her baby's limp body her heart stood still. Please don't let me lose her, she prayed, squeezing her eyes shut to prevent her tears from falling. Crying wouldn't help, she had to be strong and help Aimee in her fight for survival.

A hand reached out and enfolded her fingers in a strong grasp. Zac was hurting too, she could see it in the tense line of his jaw, but she couldn't bring herself to meet his gaze. Sympathy briefly flared for what he must be going through, the agony he must be feeling that Aimee could be taken from him so soon after she had come into his life. But when they arrived at the hospital and the ambulance doors were flung open, she forgot everything but the need to focus on her baby. Aimee needed her and there was no room in her heart for anyone else.

CHAPTER NINE

ONE week later Freya stood in the nursery, struggling to hold back her tears as she stared into the cot. Aimee was sleeping peacefully, her long eyelashes feathering her cheeks that were now flushed with healthy colour once more.

The hours after they had arrived at the hospital had been fraught with tension as the little girl underwent a series of tests, and the eventual diagnosis that she did not have meningitis had only been a partial relief. Aimee had been suffering from a virus that had taken a hold on her young body. For the next three days she had lain in her hospital bed attached to wires and monitors and despite the efforts of the excellent medical team, had shown no signs of recovery. But on the fourth day her high temperature had gradually dropped back to normal and when she'd woken from a long nap she had sat up, demanded a drink, wolfed down a banana and only been persuaded to remain in bed because her toy rabbit was poorly and needed looking after.

Aimee's recovery had been nothing short of miraculous, and now that they were back at the penthouse Freya felt as though she had ridden an emotional roller coaster. She would not have been able to get through the past week without Zac, she admitted to herself. From the moment Aimee had been whisked away by the medical team, he had been faultlessly supportive, countering her frantic fear with quiet calm and relaying every snippet of information from the doctors in an effort to allay her anxiety.

He had been a rock and she'd clung to him unashamedly, reassured by his strength and comforted by his decision to fly in one of the world's leading paediatricians. Her pride was no longer important and she was simply grateful that he could afford the best medical care for their daughter. More than anything it had brought home to her that Aimee's future lay here in Monaco, with her father.

'Come away now, *chérie*,' Zac said softly when he entered the nursery and walked silently over to the cot. 'She's sleeping soundly and Jean insists that she will sit up all night to check on her.'

'I can't believe how well she looks,' Freya muttered past the constriction in her throat. 'Just a week ago I thought…I thought I would lose her and I was so scared.' The tears were falling, despite her determination to wait until she reached the privacy of her own room before she broke down. Overwhelmed by exhaustion and relief, she could not hold back the flood of her emotions, but as she buried her face in her hands strong arms closed around her and she was drawn up against the solid wall of Zac's chest.

'It's all right, Freya, cry it out. You can't take any more and it's no wonder after the nightmare of the past week. Aimee is completely well and she'll bounce back from this in no time,' he assured her as he lifted her into his arms and strode down the hall. 'It's you I'm worried about, *chérie*. You've barely slept for days and I can't recall the last time you ate anything. It can't go on,' he told her firmly, 'and if you won't look after yourself, then I'll have to do it for you.'

Freya was beyond arguing. Zac was arrogant and bossy and usually she would have rebelled against his authority, but the hours she'd sat at the hospital, willing her baby to recover, had left her feeling as though she had been put through a mangle.

'Bed,' he stated grimly when he reached her room and set her down, his mouth tightening at the sight of her white face and the purple bruises beneath her eyes. 'Perhaps you'll look a little less like a ghost after a good night's sleep.'

'I need a bath first,' she mumbled, almost too weary to speak, but he shook his head firmly.

'You can have a bath tomorrow. You're too tired tonight; you can barely stand up. Let me help you get changed.' He held out her nightdress and moved to unfasten her blouse.

'It's all right, I can manage.' The temptation to throw herself in his arms and beg him to hold her was so strong that she bit her lip to prevent the words from spilling out. She couldn't cope with him tonight, not when her emotions were so raw, and to her relief he stood and walked over to the door.

'Call me if you need anything. *Bonne nuit, chérie,*' Zac bade her softly before he retraced his steps back to the nursery and stood watching over his sleeping daughter. A hand seemed to curl around his heart as he absorbed the beauty of her golden curls and the tiny heart-shaped face that reminded him of Freya. He loved Aimee beyond words and the days she had spent in the hospital had been the worst of his life, but now she was home safe and well and he was struggling to assimilate exactly what he felt for her mother.

Light was still streaming from beneath Freya's bedroom door when he walked past and he hesitated momentarily before giving in to the urge to check that she was safely asleep. But her bed was empty and his mouth tightened as he crossed the room to the *en suite*, recalling her stubborn expression when he'd left her. Surely she wouldn't have risked taking a bath tonight?

'Freya!' The bathroom door was locked and he rattled the handle impatiently, his unease growing when he called again and received no reply. 'Freya—what the devil are you doing in there?'

In the distant recess of her mind, Freya recognised that someone was calling her name. She felt curiously weightless, as if she were floating, but her name sounded again and with an effort she forced her eyelids open at the same time as she swallowed a mouthful of water. Coughing and spluttering, she jerked upright just as the bathroom door splintered from its hinges and Zac burst into the room.

'*Mon Dieu!* I don't believe you! You fell asleep, didn't you? Do you have a death wish or something?' he demanded furiously. He loomed over her, hands on his hips and aggression pumping from every pore as a potent mix of fear and adrenaline coursed through his body. 'I told you not to have a bath until tomorrow. Can't you ever do as you're told? You might have drowned,' he said, his voice sharp with relief.

Freya shrivelled beneath his glowering fury and sank deeper beneath the rapidly disappearing bubbles. 'I couldn't bear feeling so dirty,' she mumbled. A spark of pride brought her chin up and she forced herself to meet his furious gaze.

'The maid could have helped you if you'd waited until tomorrow morning,' he growled, 'but instead, because of your impatience, you'll have to put up with me playing nursemaid while I rub you down.'

'I don't need you or anyone else to *rub me down*; I'm not a horse!'

'*Non,* you are the most infuriating woman I've ever met,' Zac agreed tightly as he unfolded a towel and approached her. 'You're so exhausted you can barely sit up, let alone haul yourself out of the bath. A less patient man would let you sit there all night,' he added with such supreme arrogance that Freya considered inflicting serious injury with the loofah.

'I can manage,' she muttered, but as usual Zac was right. The sheer terror she'd felt for Aimee was now taking its toll and she felt limp and utterly drained. She hadn't deliberately set out to anger Zac and the sight of his grim face brought a rush of tears to her eyes. 'I need to wash my hair,' she choked miserably.

For a moment she thought he was going to ignore her, until with a muttered oath he dropped the towel he was holding and unbuttoned his shirt cuffs before rolling the material over his forearms. 'Lie back in the water and lean against my arm,' he instructed as he knelt beside the bath and slid his arm beneath her back.

Warily, Freya did as he asked. The bubbles were dispersing fast and her cheeks burned when she felt his gaze slide over her briefly. He'd seen her naked body many times before, she reminded herself impatiently, but right now she felt acutely vulnerable. 'Zac...'

'Do you want me to help you or not?' he growled, his tone warning her that she'd already pushed him to his limits. Weakly she closed her eyes and allowed herself to be soothed by the gentle motion of his hand as he massaged shampoo into her scalp. It felt so good that her muscles gradually relaxed and even the knowledge that the bubbles had almost gone, leaving her slender limbs exposed to his gaze, failed to destroy the magic of his touch.

'There, you'll do,' he said abruptly, shattering

the spell. He adjusted the water temperature and used the shower attachment to rinse her hair, his expression unfathomable as he kept his eyes fixed firmly on her face. The tension was back, a prickling, tangible force that made Freya's nerve endings quiver.

'If you could just pass me a towel, I'm sure I'll be fine,' she began, and then gasped when he scooped her out of the bath. 'Zac!' In an agony of embarrassment, she buried her face in his shirt while he wrapped a towel around her and carried her through her room and along the hall to his bedroom. 'Please—I can take care of myself,' she mumbled, but he ignored her and used the towel with brisk efficiency to rub her body until she was tingling all over.

She was going to die of embarrassment tomorrow, Freya thought sleepily, but Zac had that determined gleam in his eyes that she knew so well and it was easier to give in to him. Her eyelids felt heavy and she was barely aware of him popping her nightdress over her head. When he drew back the bedcovers she wanted to remind him that this was his room, not hers, but he ignored her small protest and tucked her between the sheets as if she were a small child.

'I know this is my bed, *chérie*,' he said with a quiet implacability in his voice that would have alarmed her had she heard it. But she was already asleep by the time he had stripped out of his clothes and slid into bed beside her. 'The time for fighting is over,' he murmured as he leaned over and brushed his lips lightly across her mouth, 'and this is where you belong.'

It was still dark when Freya awoke. Not the inky blackness of midnight, but a soft, shadowy darkness as dawn crept closer. This was Zac's room, she realised as her eyes slowly adjusted to the lack of light. She was in Zac's bed and it had been his arms holding her close throughout the night. He was still holding her, she amended when she turned her head and met a wall of warm, satin skin overlaid with a fine covering of black hairs.

The rhythmic rise and fall of his chest told her he was asleep. She shouldn't be here, and now was the ideal opportunity to slip back to her own room. But the temptation to remain close to him, cocooned in this twilight world with the man she loved, was too strong to resist. With a small sigh she closed her eyes and inhaled his clean, masculine scent. Slowly, inexorably, her senses stirred until she was conscious of each separate nerve ending tingling in illicit anticipation.

Common sense warned her to flee before he opened his eyes and saw the hunger in hers, but instead her hand curved over his heart and she felt its steady beat reverberate through her fingertips. He shifted slightly on the mattress and she held her breath, but his relaxed muscles lulled her and she could not resist allowing her hand to slide lightly down his chest and over his flat stomach. The waistband of his boxers was an unwelcome barrier that brought a halt to her exploration. But the urge to trail her fingers lower was too strong and she cautiously edged beneath the elastic, a startled cry leaving her lips when he suddenly crushed her marauding hand against his body.

'You are following a path that can only have one outcome, *chérie*,' he drawled lazily, the sensual smokiness of his voice sending a quiver of excitement down Freya's spine. 'Are you sure it's a route you want to take?'

'Yes,' she replied unequivocally, following the dictates of her heart before her head had a chance to question her sanity. He didn't love her and maybe he never would, but he cared for her. His behaviour last night had proved that, if proof were needed after the tender consideration he had shown her during Aimee's illness. His cruel rejection two years ago had broken her heart, but since he had learned that Aimee was his child he had done everything possible to try and atone for the past. Nothing was perfect, she reminded herself, and at least he hadn't made false promises he couldn't keep. The simple truth was that she only felt half alive without him. Aimee belonged here with him, and so did she.

She heard Zac draw a sharp breath and when he turned his head the brilliant fire in his blue eyes warned her that this time there could be no going back.

'Zac.' Emotion clogged her throat and he caught her soft cry, claiming her lips in a slow, drugging kiss that coaxed and cajoled until she curled her arms around his neck and responded with all the need that had lain dormant inside her for so long.

Moments before, he had been deeply asleep but now he was wide awake and so boldly aroused that Freya suffered a tiny flutter of trepidation as the solid length of his erection straining beneath the silky material of his boxers filled her with awe and undeniable excitement. Liquid heat surged through her veins as her body recognised its mate. This was her man, the only man to know the intimate secrets of her body, and already she could feel the moist warmth between her legs as she made ready for him.

'I've missed you, Freya,' he muttered hoarsely, his lips grazing a path down her throat to settle on the pulse that beat frantically at its base. With one swift movement he drew her nightshirt over her head and stared down at her slender, naked form, tracing every dip and curve with his burning gaze. He cupped her breasts in his hands with gentle reverence and kneaded them before splaying his fingers wide, his olive-gold skin contrasting starkly against the creamy whiteness of her flesh.

'Zac, please.' She arched towards him and groaned her approval when he rolled her nipples between his thumb and forefingers until they were tight, throbbing peaks that begged for the possession of his mouth. He made her wait, teasing her with his wicked touch until she slid her hands into his hair and directed his head down to her breast. The delicate flick of his tongue across the sensitive crest was so exquisite that she tensed and moved her hips in a restless invitation. She wanted him now, this minute. She felt as if she had been waiting a lifetime and she couldn't withstand another moment of his sensual foreplay when the urgency to feel him deep inside her was driving her out of her mind.

'Slowly, *mon coeur*, I want to savour every second and taste every delectable inch of you,' he promised, putting his words into action when he moved down her body and trailed his lips over her stomach. Freya gasped when he continued lower and her fingers tightened in his hair when he gently pushed her legs apart so that he could bestow the most intimate caress of all.

It was too much, sensation piling on sensation and building to a crescendo that made her writhe beneath him. 'Please, Zac, it has to be now,' she pleaded as the first little spasms caused her muscles to clench around his probing tongue.

He finally acknowledged her urgency and for a moment his own desperate need threatened to overwhelm him so that he feared he would lose control before he had given her pleasure. Muttering an oath, he dispensed with his underwear and reached into the bedside drawer for a protective sheath.

Only then could he succumb to the demands of his desire and he groaned low in his throat when he edged forwards so that the tip of his penis was rubbing against the opening to her vagina. Slowly and with infinite care he thrust into her, and then stilled while her muscles stretched around him. She felt hot and tight and he could feel the waves of pleasure building inside him, clamouring for release. But he would die rather than hurt her and he restrained himself from plunging deep into her silken heat until he felt her relax a little.

Carefully he withdrew a fraction and then thrust into her again and again, faster now as she wrapped her legs tightly round him, her soft cries urging him on. Frantically he sought to claw back his self-control and slow his pace, possessing her with strong, hard strokes until she gave a low cry and her body convulsed around him.

'Freya…' He called her name, tried to explain that he had never known such sheer pleasure as when he made love to her, but she seemed to know, just as she had always known the effect she had on him. Her soft smile destroyed the last tenuous threads of his control and he pulsed inside her, overwhelmed by wave after wave of incredible pleasure that left him satisfied and at peace.

For a long while neither of them spoke and only the steady tick-tock of the clock broke the companionable silence. Zac had rolled onto his back, taking Freya with him, and at last she lifted her head and met his slumberous gaze. 'I need to thank you for everything you've done this last week,' she murmured huskily. 'The way you cared for Aimee—and me. I'm not sure I'd have coped without you.'

'I consider myself thanked,' he replied lightly, his eyes glinting with teasing amusement when she blushed and tried to ease away from him. He prevented her frantic bid for escape by tightening his arms around her so that she was held prisoner against his chest. 'And from now on, *chérie*, I intend to devote as much of my time as possible to pleasing you so that you will need to thank me all through the night, and at least once during the day,' he added wickedly.

'That wasn't the reason why I—' She broke off, her face flaming and wriggled her hips in an attempt to free herself from his hold until she realised the effect she was having on certain parts of his anatomy.

'I'm sorry, *ma petite*—' he grinned unrepentantly '—but I have been patient for the last two weeks and now I am very, very hungry.'

'I'm aware of that,' she muttered, feeling the hard ridge of his arousal pushing provocatively against her belly. Her body instantly stirred into urgent life. It was too soon, surely? He couldn't…

He proved conclusively that he could by lifting her hips and gently bringing her down on top of him, filling her so completely that she groaned and clung to his shoulders while she absorbed each delicious thrust.

She was shocked that he could arouse her to such a heightened degree of need so soon after she had climaxed, but already she could feel exquisite spasms of pleasure rippling through her. His hands curved possessively around her buttocks, lifted and stroked the round globes and aided her in setting a sensual rhythm that quickly became a frantic drumbeat of desire. Within seconds they were at the edge, hovered there for infinitesimal seconds before finally tumbling over into the ecstasy of mutual release.

This time when Freya eased away from him, he rolled onto his side and stared down at her, his face suddenly serious. 'You are so small and fragile, but you possess an inner strength that is quite incredible, *chérie*,' he said quietly. He stroked a stray tendril of hair from her face and a warm glow filled her when she caught the flare of admiration in his eyes. 'I don't doubt that you would have coped with the traumas of the past week without any help from me. You proved during the last two years that you can deal with anything life throws at you, including bringing up our daughter alone and unsupported. But, believe me, I will support you and Aimee now,' he told her fiercely.

'I do believe you, Zac,' Freya whispered softly, 'and I agree that Aimee belongs here in Monaco with both of us. If it's still what you want, then...I'll marry you.'

'Think about it for a moment,' he commanded urgently, so intent on persuading her around to his way of thinking that her words were lost on him. 'As my wife there would be no need for you to work and you could spend all your time with Aimee instead of having to leave her at a nursery. Wouldn't you like that, *chérie*? You clearly adore her and you must know from your own childhood that she would benefit from having her mother's undivided attention.'

'Absolutely,' Freya reiterated calmly, love and tenderness welling up inside her as she watched his expression change from frustration to dawning comprehension. 'The events of the last week have forced me to see that Aimee needs the love and care of both her parents and I agree that it would be best if we were married. It's the most logical solution,' she added, proud of the lack of emotion in her voice that disguised her aching heart. All her life she had dreamed of romance and roses, moonlight and the husky avowal of undying love, but she was prosaic enough to realise that fairy tales rarely came true and she was willing to accept Zac's marriage offer knowing that it was a contract based on convenience and a mutual desire to do their best for their daughter.

'And who can argue with logic?' Zac murmured in a dry tone that masked his irrational feeling of pique. Freya had accepted his marriage proposal with as much enthusiasm and excitement as if she were making a dental appointment. There was nothing wrong with assessing the situation they found themselves in logically, he reminded himself. Freya was no longer an impressionable girl, she was an independent woman who had managed quite well without him in the past and if necessary would do so again in the future. Clearly she had weighed up the pros and cons of becoming his wife and had reached a decision based on common sense rather than emotion.

He admired her determination to do the right thing for their daughter, but he couldn't deny a certain amount of wounded pride that she viewed him as a logical solution to a problem rather than the man she was eager to spend the rest of her life with.

'So, now that you've agreed to marry me, all we have to do is decide on the sort of wedding we want,' he said smoothly, settling himself comfortably against the headboard and giving her a smile that told her of his satisfaction that he had got his own way in the end.

She was cornered, but she had stepped willingly into the trap, Freya reminded herself when her heart lurched. Their marriage would be based on sexual desire and the love they shared for Aimee, but plenty of successful marriages had been built on less. Surely with a little effort on both sides they could make their relationship work?

'I assumed you would prefer a small wedding with the minimum of fuss,' she murmured, tearing her eyes from the sight of his magnificent body sprawled on the pillows like a sultan in the midst of his harem.

'I only intend to marry once, *chérie*, and I'd like to make it a day to remember,' he surprised her by saying. 'The ceremony doesn't have to be too lavish—if that's not what you want—but I have numerous relatives and friends I would like to invite and naturally we will want to include Aimee. She'll make an adorable bridesmaid, and of course you must have a wedding dress and flowers, and a ring. I want to do this properly, Freya,' he insisted when she looked stunned by the prospect of a big celebration. 'We may not be marrying for conventional reasons, but I'm still proud that I'm making you my wife.'

He meant of course that, unlike most couples, they were not marrying for love, Freya realised, feeling her heart contract. It was stupid to feel so hurt and she gave a careless shrug, determined not to reveal that she'd be happy to marry in a barn, dressed in sackcloth, if only he loved her. 'You've obviously given the subject more thought than me so I'll leave the arrangements to you.'

She flicked back the sheets to slide out of bed, ignoring the temptation of his naked body and the sensual gleam in his eyes. Their marriage might be a convenient arrangement but they were drawn together by a fierce mutual desire. Her one fear was what would happen if Zac's passion for her died—would he still be proud to have her as his wife when he no longer wanted her in his bed? The question settled like a heavy weight in her chest and she snatched up her robe, suddenly anxious to escape him. 'Aimee's probably awake by now,' she muttered. 'I'll go and check on her.'

CHAPTER TEN

THREE weeks later Freya was still questioning her sanity at her decision to marry Zac. Undoubtedly it would be best for Aimee, but could she ever be happy, married to a man who did not love her? The only thing she was certain of was their physical compatibility, she acknowledged ruefully. The long hours of loving in his bed each night proved irrefutably that her body had been exclusively fashioned for the giving and receiving of pleasure with this one man.

When Zac reached for her she went immediately into his arms, her heart pounding with anticipation of the delight to come when he caressed every inch of her. His hands and mouth were instruments of sensual torture that he used without mercy, exploring each sensitive dip and crevasse of her body before gently parting her and stroking her until she hovered on the brink of ecstasy. Only then, when she cast her pride aside and pleaded for him to possess her, did he relent and move over her, thrusting into her with slow, sure strokes that filled her to the hilt and made her arch and writhe beneath him.

Her only consolation was that he appeared to be no less enslaved by desire. If anything, his hunger for her seemed even more fervent now than when she had agreed to marry him and his passion showed no sign of diminishing. But it was only three weeks, she reminded herself fearfully, what would their relationship be like in three months—three years?

She glanced across the crowded room, searching for his tall frame. They were to marry in a week's time and ever since he had formally announced their engagement their relationship had been the subject of frantic gossip among Monaco's social élite. Everyone was curious to meet the woman who had finally persuaded one of the principality's most enigmatic, jet-setting playboys to relinquish his freedom, and during the past weeks they had received numerous invitations to social functions.

Tonight's party being held in private rooms at Monte Carlo's famous casino was a glittering occasion—quite literally, Freya thought wryly when she studied the array of fabulous jewellery on display. Despite her designer gown and the diamond and platinum earrings that complemented the exquisite diamond solitaire engagement ring Zac had given her, she felt seriously out of place. This was not her world and she felt like an outsider amidst the other guests who inhabited the rarefied group of the super-rich.

It was a far cry from her damp attic flat in England and her life that had revolved around trying to combine motherhood, work and study while surviving on a limited budget. This was Zac's world, but it wasn't hers, and she was aware of the whispered speculation among his peers that she was a gold-digger who had used the fact that she was the mother of his child as leverage to make him marry her.

She caught sight of him standing with a group of his close friends and her heart missed a beat as she studied him, looking relaxed, tanned and toe-curlingly sexy in an impeccably tailored black dinner suit. She would never tire of looking at him, but he possessed a magnetic charm that drew admiring glances from around the room and once again she wondered what he saw in her, when other women far more beautiful than her were queuing up for his attention.

With a sigh she moved towards the group and felt a tiny surge of confidence when Zac glanced up and focused his gaze intently on her as if she was the only woman he was interested in.

'There you are, *chérie*, I've been looking for you,' he greeted her softly, sliding his arm around her waist and dipping his head to brush his mouth over hers in a brief, tingling kiss. The sensual gleam in his eyes warned her that he was planning to excuse them from the party as soon as possible and she shared his impatience. She wanted to lose herself in the private world of sensory pleasure where their loving was fierce and hard or slow and skilfully erotic, but always seemed to have an underlying tenderness that tore at her heart and let her believe, just for a little while, that she meant something to him.

'I hope you're making the most of your last week as a free man, Zac,' someone from the assembled group joked. Benoit Fournier was one of Zac's closest friends and he and his wife Camille had greeted Freya with warmth and genuine pleasure that she was soon to be Zac's wife.

'For me the next few days cannot pass quickly enough,' Zac replied with a smile that lingered on his mouth as he stared into Freya's eyes. He was either a superb actor, or he really was beginning to care for her, she thought as joy bubbled up inside her. Her brain warned her to be cautious but the expression on his face made her pulse rate quicken. Dared she hope that she could ever mean something to him? Her heart was beating so fast that she was sure he must hear it, and when he lifted her hand and pressed his lips to her fingers she knew he would feel the tremor of excitement that ran through her.

'I know how you feel. The next few weeks can't pass fast enough for us,' Benoit laughed, patting his wife's rounded stomach.

'When is your baby due?' Freya asked Camille with a sympathetic smile. She remembered how the final weeks of her pregnancy with Aimee had dragged while her nervousness about the impending birth had increased.

'Three weeks,' Camille groaned, 'but our first child was ten days late and I'm not holding out any hope that number two will appear on time. Louis is so excited about the new baby,' she confided. 'Are you and Zac planning to have more children some day—a little brother or sister for Aimee?'

It wasn't something they had ever discussed, Freya realised silently, and, faced with the question, she wasn't sure how to reply. Aimee's conception had been an accident that had had shattering consequences. Zac hadn't wanted children, but now he was devoted to his little daughter. His vasectomy had reversed and there was no medical reason why he should not father another child.

Her eyes were drawn to Camille's belly, swollen with her unborn baby, and a warm glow filled her as she pictured herself in the same

situation. She would love to have a little companion for Aimee, she mused softly, a baby whose
conception was planned and the pregnancy
shared with Zac. Perhaps she would give him a
son, a dark-haired, blue-eyed boy who would be
the image of his father.

'Aimee isn't two yet and I'd like to give her my
undivided attention for a little while longer,' she
murmured. 'But one day I'd like to have another
baby.' She turned to Zac and froze. His smile
had disappeared and the expression in his eyes
turned her blood to ice. The conversation around
them moved on to other topics but the buzz of
words seemed distant and unintelligible. It took
all her acting skills to smile and act normally, but
inside she felt sick with misery. For those few unguarded seconds Zac had been unable to disguise
his look of dismay at the idea of them having
another child, and her little flame of hope that
their marriage could work flickered and died.

The band struck up a popular tune and people
began to drift onto the dance floor. Zac seemed
to have regained his composure and glanced
down at her. 'Would you like to dance?' His eyes

gleamed wickedly. 'I have vivid memories of the last time we danced together.'

She blushed at the shaming recollection of how he had brought her to the peak of sexual pleasure simply by holding her close, and hastily shook her head. 'I need to go to the cloakroom…perhaps Camille…' Zac's eyes narrowed on her flushed face and she turned and hurried away before he could stop her, desperate to be alone for a few minutes while she dealt with the realisation that he clearly did not want another child.

Mercifully the cloakroom was empty and she splashed water on her cheeks and tried to hold back the tears that burned her eyes. Fool, she berated herself angrily. She'd known from the outset that Zac had never wanted a family and, although he adored Aimee, he had not chosen to be a father or husband. The only reason he was marrying her was to provide their daughter with a stable upbringing and, much as she might wish it, their marriage was never going to be a conventional one.

'Hello, Freya.'

A face appeared beside hers in the mirror and

Freya's heart sank. 'Annalise, how are you?' she faltered, frantically trying to sound cool and collected despite the sick feeling in the pit of her stomach. Monaco was a small place and she had steeled herself to accept that she was likely to run into the stunning glamour model at some point. It was just a pity that it was tonight, when she was already feeling vulnerable and insecure, she thought miserably.

Annalise Dubois looked stunning in a black silk sheath that was split to mid-thigh and clung lovingly to her voluptuous curves while her flame-coloured hair tumbled down her back in a mass of riotous curls. Freya was suddenly glad that Zac had insisted on buying her some new clothes. She had shuddered at the price of the peach-coloured chiffon gown she was wearing tonight, but was aware that Annalise's assessing gaze had recognised the dress was from an exclusive fashion house.

'I heard you were back,' Annalise said without preamble, her eyes narrowing on the sparkling diamond on Freya's finger. 'But I admit I was surprised to hear that you've actually managed to get Zac to marry you. A baby is *such* a useful bargaining tool. I almost wish I'd tried the same trick myself. Everyone knows Zac is too much of a gentleman to allow his child to remain illegitimate, although I understand there was some question over the child's paternity,' she intoned softly. 'Presumably Zac insisted on the necessary tests before he agreed to marriage?'

Freya couldn't prevent a tide of colour from staining her cheeks and the sick feeling was so strong it threatened to choke her. 'I'm not sure that it's any of your business,' she murmured, forcing herself to remain polite even though the knives were clearly out. 'I've never made any demands of Zac, he's free to do what he wants, and he wants to marry me.'

'For the sake of his child,' Annalise stated with an air of confidence that Freya found deeply disturbing. 'I'm glad you realise he's a free agent. Zac would never be coerced into doing something unless he could see the benefits to himself. He's obviously determined to claim his child, and of course he'll stand a better chance of winning custody of her in the future if he marries you.'

'I really don't think we should be having this conversation,' Freya said sharply. Annalise was a nasty piece of work, but her vile insinuations were pooling in Freya's head like poison being drip-fed through a pipette.

'Poor Freya, you always were such an innocent.' Annalise laughed dismissively. 'Did you know that Zac and I are lovers, or has he kept that little secret from you?' She pouted prettily at the unmistakable look of shock on Freya's face. 'Don't let it worry you darling, Zac's the master of discretion when he comes to my apartment. You don't really think he works late every night?' Her brows arched in mock surprise. 'We've had an arrangement for years that suits both of us very well. A word of warning, though,' she drawled spitefully as she inspected her appearance in the mirror. 'Zac's no pussycat and I wouldn't bank on your life of domestic bliss lasting long. He lives life on the edge and thrives on adventure—he'll hate feeling tied down and he'll soon grow bored of babies.'

She swept out of the cloakroom leaving Freya feeling so shaken that she gripped the edge of the dressing table for support. Annalise was lying, she told her reflection fiercely. Zac had made love to her every night for the past few weeks; he would have to be Superman to be sleeping with the Frenchwoman as well.

Taking a deep breath, she walked out of the cloakroom to rejoin the party and watched Annalise saunter across the dance floor, heading straight towards Zac. Nausea swept over her as she saw the glamorous model kiss him on each cheek and murmur something in his ear that caused him to smile. There was an easy familiarity between them, as if they were entirely comfortable with each other—the familiarity of lovers, Freya thought on a wave of sheer agony.

It wasn't true. Please God, it wasn't true, she thought numbly. Common sense told her there was a strong possibility that Annalise had been lying. If their marriage was going to stand any chance of success, she would have to trust Zac, she told herself fiercely. He had told her he would be a faithful husband—but maybe he had just said that to persuade her to marry him.

Was this what their married life would be like?

she brooded. Would she be slowly destroyed by jealousy and uncertainty, always looking around at parties and wondering if his current mistress was also present? The thought was unbearable and she choked back a sob as she watched Zac lead Annalise onto the dance floor.

She knew he didn't love her, but he wanted her in his bed, and she had kidded herself she could be content with that. Now she saw with blinding clarity that it would be a fate worse than death. He was the love of her life, the other half of her soul, and without him she was incomplete. But she was destined to spend the rest of her life with a gaping great wound in her heart, because he had never loved her and he never would.

Sheer willpower enabled Freya to keep a smile on her face for the rest of the evening, but by the time she slid into the car next to Zac for the short drive home her jaw was aching and her heart felt like a lead weight in her chest.

'What's wrong—do you have a headache, *chérie*?' Zac queried when he glanced at her drawn expression.

It was tempting to seize on the excuse. She knew it would evoke his sympathetic response and that the moment they reached the penthouse he would insist that she went straight to sleep rather than make love to her.

She needed to be alone tonight. Her mind was spinning and her run-in with Annalise had stirred up all her old insecurities. Was Zac against the idea of more children because he did not want to increase his links to her? she wondered, recalling his expression when Camille Fournier had asked if they would like more children. And was he sleeping with Annalise? If so, it gave her an insight on how he viewed their forthcoming marriage. Perhaps he was he intending to play at happy families while conducting a series of affairs behind her back.

'I feel fine,' she said shortly, refusing to admit that her emotions felt as bruised as her body had been after the accident that had brought Zac back into her life. It was strange to think that if she had been driving down that road a few minutes earlier the tree would not have fallen yet and she would not have crashed her car. It was likely she would never have seen or heard from Zac again, but in the course of a split second her life had changed for ever and now here she was, about to marry the man she loved and feeling as though her heart would break.

She was silent for the rest of the journey and as the lift whisked them up to the penthouse she was aware of Zac's sharp glances. Once inside, she headed straight for her room, but he caught up with her and swung her round to face him.

'You seem to have lost your sense of direction,' he drawled. 'My bedroom is along the hall. What's wrong with you?' he demanded tersely, when she simply stared up at him with huge, over-bright eyes. 'You've looked like a ghost for most of the night. Are you ill? If you won't tell me what's wrong, I can't help you, *chérie*,' he added impatiently, the gleam of frustration in his eyes telling her that he was fast losing his patience and was tempted to shake the truth from her.

The truth—that loving him was tearing her apart—was impossible to reveal. 'Nothing's wrong,' she lied. 'I'd just rather sleep on my own tonight.' Her pride refused to allow her to confront him about Annalise's allegations. If he suspected she was jealous of the glamour model, he might realise that she was in love with him and she would rather die than have him feel sorry for her.

Zac briefly considered hauling her into his arms and kissing her until he broke through the barriers she had erected, but she looked achingly vulnerable and he accepted that, for once, making love to her was not the answer. Instead he gave an angry shrug of his shoulders. 'Fine,' he snapped, 'sleep on your own, but a week from now you will be my wife and you'll share my bed every night. There will be no separate rooms, do you understand?'

'Oh, yes,' she flung at him bitterly. 'I understand that my role in our marriage will be to provide sex whenever and wherever you want it—less of a wife, more like a glorified whore. Tell me, Zac,' she demanded, her heart fluttering fearfully at the savage anger in his eyes, 'why are you marrying me? Being tied down with a wife and child is not what you really want, is it? I saw your face tonight when Camille mentioned the possibility of us having more children,' she said quietly, 'and I realise that you'll soon feel trapped by the responsibilities of being a husband and father.'

'That's a ridiculous thing to say,' he growled, but he refused to meet her gaze and despair washed over her.

'Is it? Be honest with me, Zac. A few years from now can you see yourself as a contented family man? Can you see us having other children who will be brothers and sisters for Aimee?'

The silence was agonising, dividing them as decisively as a ravine opening up between them. 'No,' he admitted heavily, and the single word shattered her.

So now she knew. But the realisation that he viewed their marriage as a temporary contract while Aimee was growing up was unbearable and with a muffled sob she spun on her heel and raced out of the door.

'Freya!' He caught up with her just as she reached her room and she shook wildly in his grasp as if she could not bear for him to touch her. 'I will be a good father to Aimee, and a good husband.'

He sounded as though he was making a state

proclamation and she could not disguise her bitterness. 'I don't doubt that you'll do your duty, Zac. I'm sure you'll take your responsibilities seriously, just as my grandmother did when she brought me up after my mother abandoned me. But I've realised that I want more than that. Is it really too much to want to be loved?' she cried. 'Is it too much to ask that one day someone will find a place for me in their heart, not because of duty or convenience, but because I'm actually special to them? Or is there something about me that fails to inspire love and affection—some genetic fault that makes me unlovable?'

Zac tensed at her words and a shutter seemed to come down over his face so that she had no idea what he was thinking. He probably thought she was a silly, hysterical mass of insecurities, she thought bleakly, and he was probably right. He had never pretended that he'd asked her to marry him for any other reason than to provide their daughter with a stable upbringing and he was looking at her now as if she had taken leave of her senses.

'You're talking nonsense,' he said quietly.

'You're tired and over-emotional. Come to bed and let me show you how good our marriage will be.'

'You mean you want sex.' Freya resisted the temptation to bury her pride and allow him to sweep her off to their special world where they communicated without the need for words. She had spent the past weeks since she'd agreed to marry him kidding herself that one day she would make him love her. It was time to face reality, but she couldn't do that while she was in his bed. 'Not tonight, Zac. I don't think I could bear it,' she whispered before she stepped into her room and shut him out.

In the morning he had gone. She was trying to persuade Aimee to eat her breakfast when Laurent informed her that Zac had been called away to deal with an urgent company matter. Freya absorbed the news silently and refrained from pointing out that it seemed unlikely he would hold a business meeting on a Sunday. She spent the day in a curiously numbed state and obligingly smiled and nodded when Yvette regaled her with the plans for their forthcoming wedding.

Zac had employed the services of a top wedding planner as well as involving his mother in organising the ceremony, which was to be held in the garden at La Maison des Fleurs. An exquisite ivory silk bridal gown was now waiting for a final fitting and Aimee was going to steal the day in a confection of pink tulle. It had all the ingredients of a fairy-tale wedding—apart from one vital fact, Freya mused bleakly. Love was missing, and, at this precise moment, so was the groom.

Sunday dragged into Monday and there was still no word from him. On Tuesday six dozen red roses were delivered to the penthouse—no accompanying note, simply a card with his name scrawled across it. Why had he sent them? she mused tearfully as she buried her face in the velvety petals and inhaled their delicate perfume. It was the first time anyone had ever sent her flowers, and she wondered if Zac had any idea how much the simple gesture meant to her. Red roses were for love but she refused to read anything into his choice of flowers. She was tired of hoping and she sternly told herself that he'd probably just instructed the florist to send a bouquet.

She missed him so much that it hurt and that night she gave up trying to sleep in her bed and moved into his, no longer caring what he might think if he returned home and found her there. The nights she'd spent without him had been purgatory, but the faint, lingering scent of him on the sheets comforted her and she fell asleep with her face pressed against his pillow.

Some time in the early hours she was woken by the faint sound of the front door closing, followed by footsteps in the hall. Zac was home and her spirits soared as she held her breath and waited for him to enter the room. She was nervous of facing him after her bout of hysteria the night before he'd left and screwed her eyes shut, hoping he would assume she was asleep. With any luck he would slide between the sheets and take her in his arms, she thought weakly as a tremor ran through her. She wouldn't reject him. Pride was a lonely bedfellow and she couldn't fight her feelings for him any more.

But he didn't come. Minutes passed and she opened her eyes and stared at the door, willing him to open it. Maybe he had poured himself a nightcap and had fallen asleep on the sofa? Unable to stand the tension any longer, she shoved her arms into her robe and crept into the hall. Aimee and the staff were all asleep and the sitting room was deserted, but a light shone on the staircase leading to the roof-garden and after a moment's hesitation she hurried up the steps.

'Zac!'

He was sitting at the far end of the pool, slumped in a chair with his legs outstretched and a bottle of cognac on the low table in front of him. He looked…wrecked, Freya noted as her eyes skimmed over his dishevelled appearance. He had lost his tie and his shirt was open at the neck, while the full day's stubble shading his jaw only added to his raw sex appeal.

'You're home,' she said inanely. 'I heard you come in and I…thought you would come to bed.' She walked around the pool towards him and gave him a tentative, hopeful smile.

Zac's eyes narrowed and he took a gulp from the glass in his hand. 'I find it hard to believe you were waiting for me, *chérie*? And I think it's probably safer for both of us if I remain here tonight.'

'So you can get drunk?' she asked sharply, glaring at him when he poured a generous measure into the glass.

'I prefer to think of it as a necessary anaesthetic,' he drawled laconically. 'I've discovered over the last few days that life is easier to cope with if you're numb from the neck up.'

'You're not making any sense.' She took a deep breath. 'What's the matter, Zac?'

He was silent for so long that she wondered if he had heard her, but then he suddenly got to his feet and sounded the death knell to all her foolish dreams when he coldly announced, 'I've decided to postpone the wedding.'

CHAPTER ELEVEN

FOR a few seconds the floor beneath Freya's feet seemed to sway and she inhaled sharply. 'I see,' she managed at last, past the constriction in her throat.

'I doubt it,' Zac murmured, and his light, almost casual tone opened the floodgates of sheer agonising pain.

'All right, I don't see, and I certainly don't understand.' She flew across the remaining few feet that separated them and halted in front of him, bewilderment, hurt and sheer fury blazing in her eyes. 'I thought we'd agreed that we could make our marriage work—for Aimee's sake.'

'I thought so too, but I realise that I can't go through with it right now,' he said grimly, a nerve jumping in his cheek as he stared down at her. The patio lights cast long shadows and she saw the weariness in his gaze, as if he hadn't slept for days.

Reaction was setting in, leaving her feeling numb. 'Why not?' she whispered, her voice cracking.

The silence shredded her nerves and when he finally spoke his voice was raw, as if his throat were lined with broken glass. 'Because I haven't been honest with you—and you more than anyone, Freya, deserve honesty.'

'Oh, no!' Pain tore through her and her hand flew to her mouth as if she could somehow hold back her betraying cry. 'It's Annalise, isn't it?' She couldn't prevent the tears from sliding unchecked down her face; her world was crumbling and her heart felt as though it had splintered in two. 'You don't have to tell me, Zac, because I already know you're having an affair with her. She took great delight in revealing your little secret when I met her at the party the night before you went away.'

His head jerked up and he stared at her as if she had taken leave of her senses. 'Don't be ridiculous. Of course I'm not having an affair with

Annalise—or any other woman,' he said in astonishment. '*Mon Dieu, chérie*, when would I find the time or the energy after spending my nights having the most incredible sex with you?'

He seemed so genuinely astounded by her accusation that Freya blinked at him through her tears. 'Annalise said…' she began falteringly.

'I don't care what she said, she was lying.' Seeing her abject misery, he made a huge effort to contain his impatience. 'We had a brief affair about six months after you and I split up, but that's all, and it meant as little to me as all my other relationships,' he told her bluntly.

Freya stared at him uncertainly. 'But why did she say it, if it wasn't true?'

He shrugged dismissively, as if he was bored of the subject of Annalise Dubois. 'Because she enjoys making trouble and I imagine because she's jealous of you.'

No one could lie so convincingly. He had to be telling the truth, Freya decided, but her spurt of relief quickly died. 'Well, if it's not Annalise, then in what way haven't you been honest with me?' she asked fearfully when his face became shuttered once more. 'If it concerns us, our relationship, then you don't have to worry,' she said as understanding slowly dawned. He must have guessed that she was in love with him and knew that he must be honest and tell her he would never return her feelings. 'I know you don't love me,' she whispered, 'and I accept that you never will.' She looked away from him and willed herself not to cry any more, but his next words brought her head round.

'But I do love you, Freya,' he said in a low voice that seemed to be torn from the depths of his soul. 'Although for a long time I did not know it. You lighten my day…my life, in a way that no other woman has ever done, but it was only when Aimee was ill and you were so distraught that I realised I wanted to hold you and protect you from hurt, because you are infinitely precious to me.

'I can't imagine my life without you,' he admitted huskily. 'Subconsciously I think I must have loved you for ever, and that's why I was so determined to marry you, but it was easier not to question my motives too closely. Instead I selfishly took pleasure in making love to you;

took everything that you gave so generously and never offered you anything in return.

'*Je t'adore, mon ange,*' he groaned, his voice throbbing with emotions, 'but loving you beyond reason doesn't make it right.' His face twisted as if he was in pain. 'I haven't been honest about *me*. There are things I should have told you, things that you have the right to know, and it would be morally wrong for me to marry you when you don't know all the facts. Don't cry, *mon coeur,*' he pleaded, wiping away a tear with his thumb, only to see it replaced with another.

'I don't understand,' she choked. She felt as though she were balanced on the edge of a precipice, looking down into the abyss. Zac had said the words she'd dreamed of hearing, but she found it impossible to believe him. He looked drawn and haggard and if he really did love her, then he clearly did not welcome the emotion.

'Two years ago I had everything money could buy and nothing that really mattered to me— until a shy English girl with green eyes and the sweetest smile turned my life upside down,' he revealed quietly. 'I was drawn to you in a way that had never happened to me before, although I told myself it was simply good sex,' he admitted harshly. 'I wasted no time in making you my mistress and, despite coping with the loss of my father, my mother's grief and an intolerable workload, I was happy.

'You made me happy, Freya, but then you dropped the bombshell that you were pregnant and I was certain the baby wasn't mine because, unbeknown to you, I'd had a vasectomy to ensure I would never father a child.'

'Zac…' The raw emotion in his eyes made her heart stand still. How could she ever have thought him cold, or believed that he didn't care? she wondered.

He shook his head and placed a finger gently across her lips. 'What I have to tell you has been burning a hole inside me for what seems like a lifetime and I need to speak now, while I have the courage.'

Fear settled over Freya like a shroud and she shivered. What on earth did Zac have to tell her that demanded his courage?

'I've already told you that I was in my teens when my mother gave birth to my twin sisters. They appeared to be healthy babies, but died when they were a few months old,' he said flatly. 'Doctors discovered that both my parents carried a gene that resulted in a high chance of their children developing a rare, incurable illness. I did not develop the disease, but my parents were advised that there was a possibility I had inherited the gene and could pass it on to my own children.'

As his words slowly penetrated her brain Freya felt her blood congeal in her veins and her legs buckled as terror swept through her. 'Could Aimee develop the illness?'

'*Non,*' Zac gripped her arms and quickly sought to reassure her. 'A child can only be affected if both parents carry the gene, and if you were also a carrier Aimee would have shown signs of the disease by now. But there is a fifty-per-cent chance that I am a carrier. I had a vasectomy because I was determined that I would be the last in the genetic link—the last Deverell. But the vasectomy reversed. When I discovered that Aimee is my child I knew she might also carry the gene and I despaired of telling you.' The lines of strain around his eyes were plainly evident and Freya's heart ached for him. He had carried the burden of worry for their child alone in an attempt to protect her.

Finally she could understand Zac's decision never to father a child and his adamant refusal to believe that the baby she had conceived was his, and now that she knew the whole tragic story she wanted to weep for him—for the young boy who had witnessed his parents' devastation when they had lost their twin daughters and for the man who had done everything in his power to prevent another child from suffering.

She looked up at him and caught the flare of pain in his eyes before he quickly masked his thoughts. He'd said that he loved her and he adored Aimee… 'I understand everything you've told me, but not why you want to postpone the wedding,' she murmured. 'If you love me…'

'More than life, *mon coeur*,' he vowed fiercely, 'more than you can ever know.' He slid his hands up her arms to cup her face and she could have died at the expression in his brilliant blue gaze, the faint sheen of moisture that revealed his vulnerability and his deep, abiding love for her.

'When I received the results of the paternity test I was desperate to know if I carry the gene and the likelihood that I had passed it on to Aimee. I contacted medical experts who specialise in genetics and discovered that in the last two years a reliable test has been developed, which means that I will finally know if I am a carrier. If I am, then Aimee will have to be tested and it will mean that I can't risk having another child,' he said in a strained voice.

He broke off and stroked a stray tendril of hair from her face with fingers that shook slightly. 'When you spoke to Camille at the party I saw in your face how much you would love another baby and it hit me like a thunderbolt that I hadn't been fair to you, *chérie*. I've spent the past three days on *The Isis* in abject despair, knowing that it would be wrong to marry you until I know if I can give you other children.

'Waiting for the test results is tearing me apart. If it proves negative then I will gladly marry you, but if it is not, then—' He broke off, his expression tortured.

Freya stared at him. 'And if it's not, what then? What are you suggesting?' she demanded fiercely. 'That I marry someone else? Have children with someone else? Is that what you want?'

'No, it's not what I want,' he denied savagely. He spun around so that his back was to her and ran a hand over his face, but Freya saw the betraying gesture and her heart clenched with love and tenderness. 'It would destroy me to see you with another man, to know that you loved him and to watch you grow big with his child whenever I came to visit Aimee. But what I want isn't important,' he continued huskily. 'I want you to be happy, *chérie*.'

'Then come here and make me happy,' she pleaded softly. 'You're the only man who can, the only man I want. I love you,' she said simply, opening her arms to him when he jerked his head round and stared at her.

'Don't you understand? I want to postpone the wedding until I know if I can give you more children.' He swallowed when she walked towards him and wrapped her arms around his waist. For a moment he fought against his desperate need to hold her, but he had never been able to resist her smile and with a groan he slid his fingers into her hair.

'I've waited for you to ask me to marry you for two long years and I'm not waiting any longer,' she told him fiercely. 'I don't care what the test reveals. Aimee is healthy and you've said she stands no chance of developing the illness herself. It would be nice to give her a little brother or sister, but I love you, Zac, and that's more important than anything else. All I've ever wanted is for you to love me the way I love you, completely and utterly for the rest of our lives.'

'Freya…' His voice broke and he claimed her mouth with such tender passion, such *love*, that her eyes filled once more. '*Je t'aime, chérie*, for ever.'

'Show me,' she whispered against his mouth and smiled when he scooped her up and carried her over to a sun lounger.

'Do you want me to take you to the bedroom?'

'No time,' she muttered thickly. She had been starved of him for the past two nights and she couldn't wait a moment longer. His clothes were a hindrance and she tugged impatiently at his shirt buttons, murmuring her pleasure when she parted the material and ran her hands over his broad chest.

He dispensed with her robe with similar speed and paused to savour the sight of her in a wisp of black lace before he drew her negligee over her head and absorbed the beauty of her soft curves. His woman—the thought of living without her had almost destroyed him and the knowledge that he didn't have to was slowly sinking in. He would make her happy, he vowed fiercely. He would devote the rest of his life to loving her so that she forgot the lonely years of her childhood and knew beyond doubt that he adored her.

He lowered his head and captured her mouth in a tender caress before increasing the pressure, crushing her soft, moist lips beneath his own as passion quickly built to a crescendo of need. Freya curled her arms around his neck and arched towards him when he trailed his mouth down her throat and over the soft swell of her breast. The sensation of his tongue stroking delicately over her nipple made her cry out.

'I love you so much, Zac,' she whispered, wondering how she could ever find the words to tell him what he meant to her. 'I've wanted to say the words for so long,' and had said them, silently, in the sweet aftermath of their lovemaking. Now she could say them out loud and she smiled when he transferred his mouth to her other breast and then lifted his head to stare down at her.

'The words are special, but I was afraid to say them, knowing that I should let you go,' he said deeply. 'Instead I tried to tell you with my body. When I kissed you, caressed you, my heart was reaching out to show you how much you mean to me. You are my life, Freya—you and Aimee. You mean the world to me.'

He moved over her and entered her with exquisite care, setting a rhythm that swiftly built to explosive passion. Freya wrapped her legs around him and revelled in his strong, deep strokes driving her higher and higher until she could take no more. As she shattered she called his name and heard his answering groan, heard him tell her again and again that he would love her for eternity. She convulsed around him, heightening his pleasure to an unbearable degree, and he finally lost control, gloriously and unashamedly and with a lingering sadness that he had dared not risk making love to her without a protective sheath.

Afterwards Freya hugged him tightly to her and stared up at the night sky. The moon was a pale orb suspended against black velvet and the stars seemed close enough to touch. She loved the weight of Zac's body on hers, but eventually he eased away from her and stared into her eyes.

'If the test results are positive…'

'Then we'll deal with it,' she said steadily. 'All my life I have longed to be part of a family and now I have Aimee; I feel closer to Yvette than I ever did to my grandmother and Jean is more than Aimee's nanny, she's become a dear friend. But most of all I have you,' she said softly, her eyes shimmering with tears as she traced the contours of his face. 'I want to be your wife, Zac, and know that whatever the future brings, we'll face it together. There'll be lows as well as highs, but there will always be love and that's all we need.'

Zac said no more, couldn't when his throat ached with emotion, but he kissed her and stroked his hands over her body, showing her without words that he would love her for the rest of his life.

Three days later they were married and their wedding day was everything Freya had ever dreamed of. A day of joy and laughter that began when she walked across the lawn at La Maison des Fleurs escorted by Laurent and with Aimee clutching her hand and skipping alongside. Zac was waiting for her beneath a bower of pink and white roses and as she approached he stepped forwards to draw her and his little daughter into his arms.

'*Papa,*' Aimee greeted him with an impish grin and drew murmurs of delight from the assembled guests when she toddled off to sit between *Mamie* and Jean, the two people she loved most after her parents.

Zac looked so utterly gorgeous in his superbly tailored wedding suit that Freya's steps faltered and she stared up at him, overwhelmed by the depth of her love. He smiled and she caught her breath at the lambent warmth in his gaze, an ache starting deep inside her when he lifted her hand to his lips and kissed each finger in turn.

'You know I will never let you go,' he murmured, his voice shaking with emotion. 'You are mine and I guard my possessions jealously, *chérie*.' He brushed his lips over hers in a gentle kiss that promised heaven and hand in hand they stepped forwards to make the vows of love that would last a lifetime.

EPILOGUE

FREYA tiptoed into the nursery and smiled at the sight of Aimee asleep in bed surrounded by her collection of teddies. At nearly four years old she was growing up to be a bright and beautiful little girl and was a devoted sister to her baby brothers.

At the other end of the room two cots stood side by side, each containing an identical dark-haired baby boy. From the moment Zac had learned he did not carry the gene that had taken such a devastating toll on his family, he had been eager for them to try for another child, and as usual he couldn't do anything by half, she thought wryly.

Luc and Olivier were now nine months old and were quickly discovering how much mischief they could get up to now that they could crawl.

Both had inherited their father's strong will and she'd had a tussle to change them into their sleep suits. Now, finally they were asleep and looked so utterly adorable that she couldn't resist leaning over to brush her lips against Olivier's velvet soft cheek and then Luc's.

'Ready?' Zac's voice sounded from the doorway and she glanced up, her heart lurching when his mouth curved in a wide, sexy smile.

'Do you think they'll be all right? We've never left them for a whole night before,' she murmured anxiously as she followed him into the hall.

'Of course they will. Jean and my mother will spoil them beyond redemption,' he assured her. 'It's about time we had one uninterrupted night.'

'Mmm, I'm sure we'll sleep well.'

'I wouldn't bank on it, *chérie*,' Zac warned her, the gleam in his eyes sending a quiver of anticipation through her. 'I have various plans for our second wedding anniversary, and none of them involve us lying still.'

He held her hand as they rode the lift down from the penthouse and walked along the quayside to where *The Isis* was moored. Freya could not help but glance at him, noting the way his black trousers moulded his thighs and his shirt was open at the neck, revealing the tanned column of his throat. He still had the power to make her heart stop and she swallowed at the lambent heat in his gaze when he lifted her into his arms and stepped aboard the boat.

'Happy anniversary, *chérie*.' He bent his head and kissed her until she was breathless before carrying her down to the lower deck. The master cabin was filled to overflowing with flowers and tears welled in Freya's eyes when she glanced around at the mass of roses and carnations.

'They're beautiful,' she whispered, clinging to him when he lowered her onto the bed. 'Where are you taking me?'

'Nowhere.' He grinned and the gleam in his blue eyes sent a tremor of excitement through her. 'At least, not yet. Later we'll sail along the coast to Antibes and have dinner there. But right now I'm not hungry for food, *mon coeur*.'

'I see.' Freya pouted. 'So I got all dressed up for nothing. Perhaps I'd better take my dress off before it creases.'

'I think that's a very good idea,' Zac murmured, sliding the straps of her dress down her shoulders until her breasts spilled into his hands. He groaned his appreciation and dipped his head to capture one dusky nipple in his mouth; tormenting her with his wicked tongue until she begged for mercy and he transferred his lips to her other breast.

She was on fire for him instantly, desperate to feel him inside her. She was glad that her body had returned to its pre-pregnancy shape and eagerly helped him to remove the rest of her clothes, her excitement mounting at the burning heat of Zac's gaze. Their lovemaking had been gentle and more restrained since she'd given birth to the twins, but tonight she sensed his urgency and knew that he would couple tenderness with fierce, primitive passion.

'You're incredible,' Zac breathed, his eyes darkening as he ran his hands possessively over her flat stomach and then lower to caress the sensitive flesh of her thighs. He stripped out of his clothes with indecent haste and came down on top of her, taking care to support his weight as he entered her with one slow thrust that filled her and made her groan with pleasure. Each deep stroke sent her higher and higher until she sobbed his name and clung to him while spasms of intense pleasure racked her body.

Still moving within her, he whispered the words she had waited so long to hear, vowing to love her and cherish her for the rest of his life, before his control shattered and he spilt into her, his big body shaking with the power of his release.

'This is for you, to celebrate the second year of our marriage,' he said some while later, sliding his arm from beneath her shoulders for a moment as he reached for a small velvet box. He slid the band of diamonds and emeralds onto her finger to join her wedding ring and kissed away her tears. 'You are my wife, my lover…' his voice faltered fractionally '…mother of my children, and the love of my life. I will love you for eternity, Freya,' he vowed, before he took her in his arms once more and proceeded to demonstrate without words exactly what she meant to him.

MILLS & BOON PUBLISH EIGHT LARGE PRINT TITLES A MONTH. THESE ARE THE EIGHT TITLES FOR MAY 2008.

———————⌀———————

THE ITALIAN BILLIONAIRE'S RUTHLESS REVENGE
Jacqueline Bair

ACCIDENTALLY PREGNANT, CONVENIENTLY WED
Sharon Kendrick

THE SHEIKH'S CHOSEN QUEEN
Jane Porter

THE FRENCHMAN'S MARRIAGE DEMAND
Chantelle Shaw

HER HAND IN MARRIAGE
Jessica Steele

THE SHEIKH'S UNSUITABLE BRIDE
Liz Fielding

THE BRIDESMAID'S BEST MAN
Barbara Hannay

A MOTHER IN A MILLION
Melissa James

MILLS & BOON
Pure reading pleasure

0408 Rom LP

MILLS & BOON PUBLISH EIGHT LARGE PRINT TITLES A MONTH. THESE ARE THE EIGHT TITLES FOR JUNE 2008.

————— ✿ —————

THE GREEK TYCOON'S DEFIANT BRIDE
Lynne Graham

THE ITALIAN'S RAGS-TO-RICHES WIFE
Julia James

TAKEN BY HER GREEK BOSS
Cathy Williams

BEDDED FOR THE ITALIAN'S PLEASURE
Anne Mather

CATTLE RANCHER, SECRET SON
Margaret Way

RESCUED BY THE SHEIKH
Barbara McMahon

HER ONE AND ONLY VALENTINE
Trish Wylie

ENGLISH LORD, ORDINARY LADY
Fiona Harper

MILLS & BOON
Pure reading pleasure

0508 Rom